Birth of a

Side Chick

By Yanee Brinks

Thank you to all of my family, friends, and fans. I love all of you.

I even thank my critics.

Table of Content

Prologue

From the day that I was born my momma always told me that I was born to be great and do great things. She is my biggest supporter and the reason that I go hard to get whatever I want. So it was no surprise when I graduated valedictorian of my high school class. No surprise when I got that degree in Criminal Justice. Again, graduating top of my class with all of the intent of becoming a Private Investigator. No surprise when I got that job at the PI firm. No surprise when I climbed the ranks and snatched that corner office from underneath my boss. Okay, yeah that might have been a little surprising only because he was so well established and I had only been here for six months. But when you're good, you're good. And it was no surprise when I acquired that new Maserati Quattroporte S Q4. I worked hard so you know I played hard and looked good doing it. Yeah my light brown skin glowed underneath the summer sky while my 5'6" thick frame and golden bouncy curls complicated my S Q4. Me and my car had curves in all the right places. This is why it was no surprise when I caught the eye of one of the finest men in the city. He wanted me and I wanted him so no surprise that he landed in my bed. Even if he is married...

See I'm about to take you back to the beginning and tell you how a sexy, sophisticated, and highly educated sista named Jalyn Monroe Clay became a damn side chick.

Chapter One

Jalyn

I woke up feeling like today just wasn't my day. I didn't want to get out of bed to do anything but the firm was waiting. So I sat up in bed and turned on the news. I tuned in to killing after killing and so much crime but after ten minutes and feeling more depressed I got up to shower.

I walked into the bathroom and began washing my face. Still not feeling completely awake I stepped into the hot stream and let the water massage my tense muscles. This was just what I needed. This was ecstasy.

I let my mind roam as I inhaled the relaxing aroma of eucalyptus. Yes, I'm old school and hang it from my shower head. It helps with so much. But this was just what I needed to get my day started.

As I stepped out of the shower and looked in the mirror I couldn't help but to compliment the woman starring back at me. "I must say sista that you are definitely eye candy." So why was I single?

Yeah I was 5'6", light brown skin, with ass and breast for days and still single. Although it wasn't that no one was interested. I didn't have time for the games dudes played.

So as I stood there oiling my skin making my golden complexion glow I thought about what to do to my hair. I decided that I didn't have the time to re-curl my golden curls that were now drooping thanks to my relaxing shower. I put my shoulder length hair in a bun and proceeded to get dressed.

Since my mood had changed I decided to wear something nice. Call me cheap but Anne Klein was my go to for simple yet chic. Although at three hundred dollars a suit I'd say they were anything but cheap.

No matter what anyone else thought I absolutely loved her pantsuits. I put on my single button black pantsuit tailored to hug me in all of the right places. Then I found a simple white blouse with matching black and white Anne Klein pumps. Now I was ready to go.

Now here is why I took so much time combing over my appearance because as I walked into my garage I saw a beauty waiting for me. Yes, my blue Maserati Quattroporte S Q4 was awaiting me. I had to look good to match this beauty. I am a cheap person and always shop around for discounts but I had to go all out for my car. So I jumped into my car and let the luxury take me away.

I headed up I-270 to I-64 lost in my music until I reached S Mason rd. That's when I had to bring myself back down to reality. A young black woman driving a nice car in these parts of St. Louis definitely caught law enforcements attention. Moments later I pulled up to the firm and a wave of emotions passed through me along with a sense of accomplishment.

I was overjoyed and re-energized just seeing this place. Just to know that I did it. I finished school and obtained my license. I landed my dream job shortly after that then I fought for my place in this firm and I love my job. I absolutely love it.

Even though the job can get a little stressful and dangerous at times I wouldn't trade it for anything in the world. Only thing that I'm working to change is the name on the front door. Instead of Meeble & Associates I want it to say Meeble, Clay, & Associates. Or maybe just Clay & Associates. Yeah, I like that last one the most.

I walked into the firm and was greeted by the wonderful smell of donuts and lattes. You might as well have moved my desk into the conference room that held the delicious treats because I was always drawn to them. Everyone knew this and if they wanted my attention they would meet me at this table; everyone except Margaret.

We all have that one hater at work and she was definitely a pain in the ass for me. See Margaret was a Meeble so she didn't want some black Barbie in charge. And she was salty that I took her father's top spot. But all that Margaret was good for was sucking up all of the men in the office.

I proceeded to the conference room to get my morning sugar rush. Just as I said earlier someone was already waiting on me by the treats. Matt was my superior but if he wasn't he could definitely get it. He was 6'4" tall. Matt had a nice body, short wavy dark hair, with the most beautiful blue eyes that I've ever seen. This man was gorgeous!

Matt smiled at me and said "Good morning Suga". I smiled but not because of his greeting. No, it was because he flashed the brightest set of teeth when he smiled. I'm telling you that if I had a dick it would be rock hard. This man made working here a challenge in more ways than one.

I finally broke my thoughts and said "Good morning Boss". That was my way of keeping things professional and by the smirk on his face he knew it too. Matt walked up to me not leaving much room between us. Damn he smelled so good! Then he handed me a folder that he had been holding. It was a new assignment.

I extended my hand and accepted the job. Matt broke the silence between us by saying "Have fun with this one because she's a nutty one".

I said "So why give her to me? You know that I have more important things to do with my time. Why not give it to Michelle?"

He walked away smiling but not explaining why he gave this case to me. I gathered my breakfast and headed to my office. Once I made it to my office I settled into my oversized desk chair and started up my computer.

While I'm not a huge social media fan I did take time every morning to get my daily dose of ratchetness. Looking over these profiles and eating breakfast was a habit that I needed to break. I killed an hour of my day everyday doing this.

Once I logged out of all accounts I vowed to myself to make a change starting tomorrow. For now I needed to brief myself on this new assignment.

Chapter Two

Jalyn

I buried myself in my work for the next three hours before feeling like I needed a break. See once I got going with something I couldn't stop. Wouldn't stop. It is not in my blood. Giving it my all was what I did. Especially when the case was as odd as this one.

Matt was right when he said this lady was nutty. This case had me watching two different people. My client was a married woman that wanted to make sure that neither her husband nor boyfriend was cheating on her. Can you believe this shit?!

I had to meet this lady because she was my client but I really wanted to meet this playa. After calling my client to schedule an appointment to meet with her I headed out for a brief walk. One of the perks of the job is that I'm free and required to leave the office often.

I shut my door and told Stacey, the receptionist, that I would be out of the office for a while. Once on the go I pulled out my phone and checked my notifications. One missed call, 8 new messages, and a ton of new emails.

I started with the missed call from mom but quickly ended it before it could ring again. I love my mom but I usually needed a drink when talking to her so that call would need to wait. Next, I went through my emails. Thank God none of them needed a response of any sort.

That left me with my text messages. Two were from my mom about song titles and recipes. A quick response to mom and moving on. Four were from my friend McKenzie aka Mac. I would definitely need more time to respond to those so I left them unread. One text was an appointment reminder and the last one caught my eye.

It was a text from a good friend of mine that I talked to occasionally but his text was a little different. It simply said "What's up sexy?" This was odd because out of our fifteen year friendship he had NEVER called me pretty. Naturally I was ready to blame his baby momma for this random ass text because he didn't talk to me this way.

Feelings aside I replied "Hey, what's up?" He replied instantly. At first his text seemed normal then they became a little alarming again. I finally said "Malik is everything okay?" No response. By now I had reached the park not far from the firm.

I sat on the bench thinking what could be troubling Malik. We had been friends for fifteen years and always kept in touch but that's as far as it goes. Don't get it twisted though. Malik was very sexy and a great man but our friendship had become strained over the years because of my disgust for his baby momma.

She was nothing more than a gold digger and everyone saw that but Malik. Aside from that we had a great relationship and had nothing but great vibes between us. Hell I'll be honest. I had fantasized about him plenty of times while I played with myself. Hell I'd even fantasized about him while with being with other guys. But he never expressed interest in me so I kept my feelings to myself. Plus he was in love already.

I sat in the park for half an hour just lost in thought before beginning my walk back to my office. Music playing on my phone and the cool air on my skin made me relax my mind.

I'm sure that whatever is bothering Malik is fine.

I made my way back to my desk and checked my messages. Seeing that I had nothing new I called it a day and went home to rest up for the real work tomorrow. Once I was in the car I called my girl Mac. "Hey girl, I got your messages but didn't have time to read them. What's up?"

She started with "Girl I hope you got time to talk because this nigga is trippin". That right there told me that this was going to be juicy.

I told her "Girl I'm on my way home but I can pick up a bottle of something and come by your house. What are we drinking?" She yelled "Yesss! Anything strong because I need to drink this day away." I was now on my way to the liquor warehouse for a bottle so that my girl and I could let loose.

Chapter Three

Malik

Today was such a relaxing day. Maybe too relaxing of a day because thanks to this drink in my cup I had rattled the nerves of my good friend Jalyn. I had texted her with the intent of telling her a secret but now I didn't know if I could. Right now I needed another drink.

Jalyn was waiting on me to respond to her text. Should I do it? Would she judge me? Would this hurt our friendship? I had too many questions for myself right now so I put down my phone and decided to go out with my gal. Me and my gal went out to eat dinner at a quiet little diner. I was hoping that this would take my mind off of things for a while.

It did for a while and it helped that I saw on Jalyn's social media feed that she too was out. That meant that she was too occupied to trip off of me and she was unable to listen to me too. Cool. Meanwhile my gal was talking a mile a minute about shit that I didn't care about.

I pretended to listen but she was making my head hurt. I knew for sure now that I needed to talk to Jalyn. Yvette stopped talking and looked at me. She said "What's wrong with you? You're quiet."

I replied "Nothing baby. I'm just listening to you. Ain't that what a good man is supposed to do?"

Her smile told me that I said the right words. She went back to talking but this time about us. Yvette asked "So when we get married can I quit my job?" I don't know what made her say that shit but I said no quicker than I realized. She wasn't upset by my answer because she knows that I will hold down my house regardless. But that wasn't going to work.

Yvette kept talking and I went back to thinking. This time my thoughts were on me and my gal. Was I ready for this? Was Yvette ready for this was the bigger question? I couldn't focus on any of this wedding crap until I talked to Jalyn. Besides I hadn't even proposed to Yvette's ass yet. She was bugging out.

My thoughts were everywhere right about now. I started taking and posting pictures of my gal and I across all of my social media accounts hoping that the comments would distract both of us for a while. It worked like a charm too. Comments poured in from all directions. I never understood why so many people were consumed with other people's lives and image.

This shit was sickening to me but just like everyone else I had many accounts. I was currently watching the likes build and Yvette was finally quiet. Being seen and fake praises was her thing so she would be happy for a while but to keep the momentum going I had one more stop to make.

We left the restaurant and headed to this little flower shop. We went in and I watched as the ladies made my gal a nice bouquet to take home. Yeah I love her and try to spoil her every chance that I get. Sometimes I do a little too much but you only live once.

As we walked back to the car I watched her hug and cradle those flowers with the biggest smile on her face. Just then my phone rang snapping me from my trance. I checked my phone and saw that I had a text from Jalyn. As much as I needed this conversation it had to wait until I got my girl home.

Yvette began rubbing my leg and thanking me. "Baby I love you and thank you for this wonderful evening out. Let me show you a little love." Just then she grabbed my dick and started unzipping my pants. When I saw her shift in her seat I knew that shit had just got real.

I needed some good head right now. I needed to bust one bad. But instead of head Yvette gave me a hand job. Man, I thought about telling her to stop but if she could make me nut then bring it on. Fantasies started playing in my head while I was driving. Sex. I needed sex bad.

Shit was getting out of control so I hit the gas hoping that I wouldn't get pulled over for speeding. Speeding through South County was dangerous but I needed to get home fast. We made it into the garage but not the house. She had me ready to go!

As I pulled into the garage Yvette was hopping out of the car before I hit park. I jumped out and grabbed her by her hair then bent her over. Her hands on the wall and legs spread wide for me to kill that shit from behind. It didn't take long with me replaying her handjob and my fantasies over in my head. Yeah moments later I was gripping her ass and going hard while I released everything that I had into her.

I could tell that she was in shock but I was too shocked myself to care whether or not her shock was good or bad. I had never gone hard with Yvette like that and the look on her face was sending me mixed signals about the experience. She didn't say a word. She simply kissed me and walked away leaving me to come back to reality. Back to remembering why I needed a drink and Jalyn.

Chapter Four

McKenzie

"Girl I can't believe this muthafucka here. He done pissed me off for the last time." This was why I couldn't stop drinking. I was so happy that Jalyn had come through with that bottle. My boo was tripping and it was stressing me out in a major way.

I grabbed the bottle and poured me and Jalyn a glass. She was such a bomb ass friend. Here listening to me complain about this fool and brought me a pick me up. Although she seemed a little distracted she was still helping me out more than she knew it.

"So girl he won't answer my calls. I don't know what to do. I'm so tired of chasing behind this grown ass boy. I need something real in my life."

Jalyn held up her glass and said "Amen to that shit! But for real tho Mac you need to get over him and move on to doing you. Shit, go on a few dates or something." She was right. I needed to let this dead ass relationship go.

I was holding on to a loveless and mentally abusive relationship with this idiot. And he ain't even deserving of the effort. I told her "Girl you right. I'll make that happen as soon as I talk to his ass. But when I do you need to be ready to go out because you need something hot in your life too."

Jalyn started laughing but I could tell that statement bothered her. She was fire so I don't know why she was afraid of being with a guy that was just as fly. Then I caught a glimpse of what she was looking at on her phone. Maybe that was what had her ass so distracted.

He was not my type but still a hottie. I yelled "Oh shit! I spoke too soon huh? You already got something. Why hide something like that?" She finally put down her phone and closed the picture that she was looking at.

She said "Nah that's my friend and I'm starting to worry about him that's all. He texted me earlier on some different shit and I ain't heard from him anymore. But I'm good girl. So when are we going out? I'm ready."

She had changed the subject too quick but I'll let it go. I told her that we could go out this weekend to a little bar since she didn't do crowded places. Jalyn seemed down with that and I was happy because I knew this was going to be fun.

Just as we were discussing the details of our plans my phone went off. It was more messages from my social media account.

These dudes were so thirsty it was ridiculous. But I checked them anyway. I proceeded to show my girl some of the messages that these dudes had sent me.

We laughed so hard for hours at them. Sometimes she would go on her own account and make statements related to some of the messages we had read. Then we went live and gave advice on how not to approach females. The comments from those watching were hilarious.

Of course a few people got all offended and wanted to argue their point. But see what they didn't realize was that we didn't care and that we had been drinking all night.

After we ended our live stream I thought that would have cooled off my messages. Wrong. A few kept going. I gave one of them my number because he actually seemed decent plus he was fine as fuck. I started telling Jalyn about the guy and she said "Wait a minute.

You've been clowning all night yet you ain't dumped that boy you call your man yet."

I burst out laughing but she was right. Since he wasn't worthy of my time I sent him a text that read *"Hey I was thinking...You should just stay at your home...Indefinitely...It's over"*. After thirty minutes I was expecting him to come over upset or call me yelling but I got neither.

Instead he texted back an hour later a picture of him having dinner with another chick and the subject "cool". First of all who the hell still uses a subject heading in a text!? But I was so relieved to know that I could finally move on with my life. I just hope that he was serious.

I was over the heartache, the lies, and all of the games that he played with me. I was ready for this to end.

Chapter Five

Jalyn

I had a blast at Mac's house but it was time for me to go home. We had completely drunk the whole bottle of vodka and had insulted many lame guys. Once I stood up to say goodbye I knew that I needed a ride home.

I was fucked up. I ordered an Uber and headed to the bathroom. Once I was in the bathroom I guess the liquor had me feeling myself. I began posing and taking pictures. Hell I needed a man to even send them to but that didn't stop me nor did me leaving the bathroom as I continued to take pictures as I left the bathroom.

Mac saw me and fell to the floor laughing. She said "Girl let me help yo ass out." She started taking the pictures for me then we both ended up taking pictures. The only difference was that she had someone to send her pictures to.

Our photo session was cut short by the arrival of the Uber. As she walked me out we took one last photo. This time it was a silly picture in front of the driver. He was a good sport about it and even posed with us. I told Mac that I would get my car tomorrow and we hugged goodbye.

On the ride home I texted Malik one last time then jumped on the book. I saw that I had a lot of new friend request thanks to me and Mac acting an ass tonight. I didn't care so I accepted all of them then I did something that I normally didn't do.

I found myself checking Matt's page. Ooh this man was sexy. Before I knew it I had sent

Matt a text with one of my pictures and the kissing face emoji. His response shocked me. It read "Are you drunk?" To which I replied "I might be..."

Matt said "Will you regret this in the morning"? And before I could type and send my next smart remark Matt sent his text. He was quick. It read *I'll be at your house in 15.* All I could do was smile. Yeah I said that I would never cross that line with him but I was horny as hell and I wanted some dick.

It had been almost a year since I'd let anyone touch me. Thinking of what Matt could do to me had me hot. I had closed my eyes and began fantasizing until I felt the car stop. I was finally home. And Matt was there too.

He smiled and said "I figured I'd beat you here". Then he leaned into me and whispered "Thank you for not driving". I walked past him leading him into my home and hopefully more really soon. Once inside the door I wrapped my arms around his neck and started to kiss Matt.

He grabbed me by my waist and began to kiss me back. Matt took control slowing my deep and shallow breathing down to a more passionate kiss. The way that his tongue invaded my mouth had me wondering if I could really handle him.

Breaking my thoughts but not our kiss his hands grabbed my ass and slid down my legs as he lifted me up. I wrapped my legs around his waist as he carried me to my bed and laid me down. My legs still wrapped around his waist so he was now between my legs as I was now on my back still engaged in our kiss.

Matt stopped kissing me and we locked eyes as we were in this intense stare he began to remove my heels. Taking time to massage my feet then he began removing my shirt. He caressed my breast then moved down to my pants. Once those were off Matt just stood there looking so damn good.

I was so wet. Then he told me "Jalyn I would love to devour you but not under these conditions. I want you to feel every lick, every stroke, and remember everything that I say and do to you. Baby you're so worth it. Maybe I'll get this opportunity another time".

And just like that he covered me up and said get some rest. I sat up confused by everything that just happened yet I understood and respected his decision to not take advantage of my drunken advances. Matt said "If you like I can stay until you fall asleep".

I replied "No but thank you. I mean for everything but I promise I'll be just fine". Matt kissed me one last time before walking out towards the door. I let him leave before I got up to lock the door. That man was truly something else.

Chapter Six

Malik

After going hard in the garage with Yvette I got back in my car just to think about life. Was I ready for the next move I was about to make? I took out my phone and finally responded to Jalyn's text. "Hey, wanna meet for a drink?" Jalyn replied that she had one too many drinks already and that she didn't have her car anyway.

She said "I'm home Malik and you seem troubled. You can come by my house". The next text had her address in it so I started my car and left. Even though my nerves were everywhere I was headed to her house. I put my tunes on and left my thoughts alone.

I didn't need them bothering me right now. On top of everything else I was excited. We were good friends but I hadn't seen her so tonight I was determined to let nothing interfere with seeing my friend. Once I arrived at her house I texted her that I was outside then silenced my phone. Like I said I needed this conversation and nothing was going to stop that.

Jalyn texted back that the door was open and to come in. I did as instructed. Once I closed the door and turned around I was in awe. Her place was so immaculate. It suited her in every way but to me it said that she was achieving her goals. She was making something of herself and it showed. I was so proud of her.

Jalyn walked out to the living room glowing. She had on a white satin dress that stopped mid-thigh and made her look angelic. "Well you look great. How are you?" She smiled and did a spin before walking up to me. She gave me a big hug and said "Thank you. I'm a little buzzed but I'm good. Question is how are you?"

Still hugging her I inhaled her wonderful scent and exhaled before answering. "I'm alright besides the million thoughts going through my head." She nodded and said "Yeah let me get you a drink so that you can start talking". I laughed and yelled behind her "Bout damn time! I'm ready".

Jalyn poured me a glass of Vodka then she grabbed a throw blanket and headed to the sofa where we got comfortable. "So what's up" she asked in a friendly voice. I took a deep breath and started talking. "First, I need to address the text from this morning".

"Oh shit! There's more than one issue bothering you?"

"Yeah" Then I lowered my head.

"Okay so the floor is yours".

I gathered my courage and managed to say. "Jalyn I find you sexy as fuck. I've had these feelings for you for some time but wasn't going to say anything. But tonight...Fuck! I just couldn't hold it in anymore. There's no way that I could have said my next issue without confessing that".

I could tell that she was trying to process what I said. She got up and poured herself a drink and refilled mine. I said "I thought you were done drinking tonight?" She replied, "I was but I need one to get through this night. You just blew my mind".

"Nah but I can do that." I got up and stood in front of her. I don't know what had gotten into me but we were now toe to toe. Eye to eye. Our lips met and she lost her mind. The shock made her not engage at first but once I began to pull away she wasn't having that.

Jalyn wrapped her arms around my neck and began kissing me back. Her tongue tasted good. It felt good too. I wondered what her other lips tasted like. Jalyn started to walk backwards towards her room as if she could read my thoughts.

Still engaged in our kiss I reached for her dress to remove it. She had the sexiest body and it was covered by the sexiest matching lace bra and panty set. I grabbed her back up in my arms and started to kiss her as I laid her down. I wanted her so bad.

But was Jalyn sure that she wanted me. As I paused to admire my friend before we crossed that bridge into lovers territory she spoke. She said "Malik I love you. Always have and always will. You belong to me." Hearing her say that sent me over the edge.

She helped me remove my shirt as I climbed between her legs. I never would have thought that needing my friend and wanting to talk to her would have led to this but I wasn't going to stop. Jalyn was about to be mine.

Maybe it was the liquor or maybe she was bringing out something in me. I removed her panties and started to play in her wetness. Kissing her lips then her neck until I had kissed and licked a trail down to her puddle. She was so wet.

I didn't hesitate to plant kisses on her clitoris then I licked and sucked her pussy. I feasted on her like she was my last meal. Going in and out of her while she moaned. Hell she was screaming my name and burying my face deeper in her pussy.

I didn't stop. Not until she had multiple leg shaking orgasms. Once Jalyn grabbed my head and pulled me up I knew I had satisfied her. Her bed was soaked and I loved that she tried to drown me. But Jalyn wasn't finished just yet. She wanted the dick.

As bad as I wanted to give it to her I knew that I had been with Yvette earlier. I caressed her and kissed her thighs. I kept kissing until I made it back to her lips. I whispered to her "In due time". We laid there holding each other and kissing occasionally until she fell asleep.

After she was sound asleep I cleaned myself up and headed home. There's no way that I had the heart to tell her that I had wanted help in picking out a ring for Yvette.

Chapter Seven

McKenzie

I hadn't heard back from my now ex-boyfriend so life was going good so far. Thank God that we didn't live together. I didn't have to see him ever again. Things were starting to look up for me too. Ever since Jalyn had left I had been texting with the cutie from my inbox.

He was sexy with no kids and could hold a conversation. Shit he was winning! We had made plans to hang out tomorrow. A sort of day date. For now I needed sleep. So I called it a night because I knew tomorrow would be busy.

After a good night's sleep I awoke feeling like a brand new person. Even though I had a hangover I showered and got dressed in something warm yet cute for this fall air. A cute pumpkin colored dress that mimicked a pea coat with some knee high boots.

Breakfast was going to be quick and light because I was to meet Jalyn. She lived on the go. We met at a quiet little café not far from my house. Surprisingly it was very busy this morning. It took us fifteen minutes just to get a table but once we did the tea started flowing.

I went first with telling Jalyn about my night of texting with Cordell. She read through our messages last night. She smiled and said "Looks like a keeper! Girl I'm happy for you. Shit, no kids either!?! Maybe y'all can make something happen and give me some nieces and nephews".

This hefa was beyond crazy. "Slow the fuck down Sis! I just met him and I like the baby making process but no thank you on the babies but we do have a date in a few hours". Jalyn seemed happier than me about Cordell. She said "That's why yo ass look so pretty and shit. I knew it wasn't for me. But if you have a date why the hell are we here having stupid ass scones?" We both started laughing.

"Girl family first. I had to make sure you were alright after you left drunk. I tried calling you to make sure you were okay." She shook her head and I knew she had something on her mind. "Spill it sister".

Jalyn said "I'm such a whore. I sent pictures to Matt who showed up, made out with me, put me to bed and then left me to go to sleep. Except I didn't sleep." I was looking at her in pure shock. Not because of what she did but with whom she tried it with.

Her boss was always off limits to both of us. Now I know that she was wasted last night but I needed answers. I asked her "So what happened?" Her answer was short and sweet. She said Malik happened.

Now I'm really confused and ready to cancel my date to hear these details. I gave her a side eye and Jalyn started spilling the tea. What she was saying had me sitting with my mouth open. Literally. Jalyn reached over and closed my mouth for me. I couldn't do anything but laugh and flick her off.

"About damn time that you released some tension and y'all finally let that shit out. So when do we have a party? And when did he dump Yvette gold digging ass?" Hearing Yvette's name must have struck a nerve because she yelled out "FUCK!" for the entire café to hear.

Jalyn stated "Can we finish this conversation in the car? I need to get to work and you have a date". And just like that we left. I drove Jalyn back to her car. On the way she explained that they never got to talk about what was bothering him so she assumed they were still together.

Listening to my poor friend gave me good questions to ask Cordell. I needed to know everything upfront and if he wasn't okay with that then this was over before it started. I dropped Jalyn off at her car and hugged my friend goodbye.

"I can come by your office later if you want me to."

"Nah I'm good girl. Have fun. I got some catching up to do at work."

With that I was off to my date. Everything in me was ready to get back into the real world of dating so I was praying that this guy was on the straight and narrow. Me and my girls had already ran his name through a few background checks. All checked out clear.

As I got closer to the restaurant I could feel the butterflies fluttering about in my stomach.

I sat in the car checking my makeup and hair as I gave myself a pep talk. That's when I noticed this tall dark and handsome man walking into the building.

Oh my gosh! He looked even better than his photos. I gathered myself and noticed a familiar face. What the hell was he doing here? It was my stupid ass ex, Steve. "You look good Mac. Who you meeting here? I know it ain't the prompt and pretty princess Jalyn. She would've been here before you."

He continued "I know it ain't none of your other friends because most of them are either broke or don't have a car. So who is it?"

I got out of my car and kept walking hoping that Steve wouldn't follow me inside and embarrass me. He did. Cordell saw what was happening and came over although what he did left me standing there with my mouth open.

Chapter Eight

Jalyn

I was so happy to be back in my baby. Leaving her was hard but I knew she was safe. As I headed toward the highway to get my day started I had to get my music right. Tory Lanez – Shooters was blasting through my speakers causing me to get live.

Music was my therapy. Well that and sex. And after last night I needed therapy, real therapy. I had tried not to think about how Matt would react because honestly this wasn't the first time that we almost crossed the line.

No, I was more worried about how Malik was handling it because he was madly in love with her. I was good and would pretend nothing ever happened if I saw him right now. Call me what you like but I didn't do anything nor did I ask for it.

As I pulled into my parking spot I noticed Matt sitting in his car. I got out and flashed a smile and gave a salute. He got out and in regular Matt fashion said "Morning Suga". All I could do was shake my head and laugh. But just as I thought nothing had changed between him and I. Business as usual.

Today would be a busy day for me because I was meeting with my client. Just like any other day I sat at my desk and checked all of my social media. Nothing major. Just more sad, confused, and depressed post. But before I could log out I saw a picture of Malik and her.

They looked so happy and just like that the evil crept into my soul. I commented "Truly adorable" with the heart eyed emoji. I was going to hell but I didn't care. I didn't do it because of last night but because she was just wrong for him. No matter what at the end of the day he was still my friend.

As I was laughing at my ignorance Margaret walked into my office saying that I was needed in Matt's office. She seemed amused but I didn't care. Her job was more unsecure than mine. When I entered he was on the phone and motioned for me to have a seat. I complied.

He seemed upset with whoever he was talking to. Once he finally hung up he had his head in his hands rubbing his temples. I said "I can help with that". I got up and began massaging Matt's temples. He seemed so stressed.

He grabbed my hand and kissed it. He said "I wanted you so bad last night. Will you give me another opportunity"? What the hell was going on?! Is this why he called me into his office? It was time to get what I wanted.

I leaned over and whispered into his ear "I would rather have an actual date first. Sober of course. Then we can finish last night". I stood up and smiled. Even though I had been with Malik last night I hadn't fucked him and I was horny.

Matt kissed my hand again and turned toward me in his chair. He said "Tell me you're free now and I'll take you wherever you want to go".

"My client has thirty minutes to show up before I have Stacey call to reschedule with her." He got mad all over again. He screamed "Oh Lizette can take that bullshit case. I just wanted to mess with you. So give her your file and meet me at my house in two hours".

I started walking backwards towards my office. Once I reached the door of Matt's office I turned and smiled. Seems like my life was becoming more interesting. I gave Lizette the papers that I had on her new client. She seemed confused and normally I would have stayed to explain every detail but not today.

I wanted Matt. So I left without any extra small talk. I got in my car and headed home to freshen up and find something sexy for Matt. I couldn't believe I was about to cross the line with my boss, again. Shit after last night I needed some dick and Matt was offering.

When I arrived home I showered then curled my golden locks back into the beautiful bouncing spirals they were before my shower. Even though I saw this man often and he knew what I looked like I wanted to wow him.

So I pulled out this sexy black fitted teddy that I could wear underneath clothes. I was going to wear this under my body-con dress with some stilettos. What the dress looked like wasn't important because I cared about his expression when it came off.

Then I topped it off with the amazing aroma of my body oils. Just as I looked over myself for approval I heard my phone go off. It was Matt. "Can't wait to see you beautiful". With that I grabbed my handbag and headed for my ride.

On the ride there I listened to a little music to get my head right. From Levert to Breezy I let the tunes carry my thoughts away. Honestly I didn't need them for that. Matt was sexy and I had wanted to devour this man for some time.

I pulled into his driveway with time to spare. With his top of line security he noticed immediately and texted me to come inside and get comfortable. His house was huge and gorgeous for a bachelor. There were marbled floors, Roman columns, bright chandeliers, and beautiful color schemes in every room. I guess hard work at Meeble & Associates did pay off.

As I toured Matt's home I started to follow a delicious smell. That's where I found Matt and I knew that this was really about to go down.

Chapter Nine

Malik

I hadn't talked to Jalyn about what I really wanted to but hell I hadn't talked to her period after devouring her sweetness. I wanted to do more to her but I didn't want to overstep my boundaries.

I can't lie I had fallen asleep thinking about her and woke up with the same thoughts. But all of that aside how could I ask her to help me plan a proposal now? I guess I was solo on this quest now. Maybe it was a good thing too.

Maybe now I would focus more on Yvette rather than if Jalyn approved of everything or what she was really thinking of my decision. I got up and showered trying to get my day started but as I washed my body I couldn't help what came next.

I had to do it. I stroked my dick while thinking of last night. Then new thoughts popped into my head like me entering her and fucking her sweet pussy. Right before I would cum I would fuck her pretty little mouth and end with a facial.

These thoughts sent me over the edge and I had to grab the wall as I came hard. This shit had me going insane but I had to keep going. Feeling better and out of the shower I got dressed and headed to the Hidden Gem jewelry store to buy my gal the most beautiful ring that I could.

I did feel alone standing in this store with no Jalyn or Yvette to ease my nerves. I managed to pick out a beautiful bridal set for her. Princess cut stone with two eternity bands to compliment the set. It was nothing too flashy but perfect for my gal.

Having just made a major purchase that would be changing my life I figured that I needed a drink so I called my boy to meet me. He agreed to meet me at a bar close by called Under The Table. This was a good spot for privacy. I should know because I'd brought a couple of chicks here.

Arman was my boy and I needed to share my big news with someone. When he arrived we threw a couple of drinks back and shared some laughs. It was much needed too. Now that we had loosened up a bit I decided to break the good news.

"So Arman you know that I had wanted to propose to Yvette, right?" He nodded. I pulled out the box and opened it. He choked on his beer and his eyes got big. "Damn! I knew you loved her but not that much. How much did that rock set you back?"

I took a minute to respond. I didn't care about telling him how much but I was offended by his statement on how much I loved Yvette. I looked him in his face and said "A few grand but she's worth much more". He must have caught my drift because he changed his tone.

Arman sat up straight and gave me back the ring before saying "Aye my dude, congratulations. That's a big deal. So when do you plan on popping the big question"? By now he was smiling. I shrugged and said "I don't know. It'll be a few months".

"Why so long?" He asked

I let out a deep sigh and started to explain my situation. "Bruh I love Yvette but I'm not trying to rush a lifetime decision. Besides I've been wondering if I'm even ready. Last night I fucked up." I lowered my head and I heard him say "Oh shit! Was it that chick from yesterday"?

"Nah.   You know my friend Jalyn...her."
Arman jumped up from his chair and did a
walk around the bar before coming back
yelling at me.   He said "Bruh how the fuck did
you hit that? Y'all been friends for hellas! Why
now? Aye she fine as fuck"!

He was being extra but he was right about
one thing.   She was fine as fuck.   I spent the
next couple of hours telling Arman everything
from what happened to how I was feeling at the
moment to the wedding and just life.

It felt good to vent and get some positive
feedback too.   He told me that he agreed that it
wasn't time to get married yet.   Arman said
that I needed to finish things up with Jalyn
first.   I agreed. We hadn't really talked about
anything and it was needed.

I thanked my homie for the advice and we
called it a day.   Since I was feeling better
mentally I surprised my gal at work for lunch.
She was definitely surprised that I took time to

make her feel special drunk and all. I wanted her to know that she was my number one.

We sat enjoying each other's company and laughing like high schoolers until she had to return to her shift. I didn't want to ruin our good vibes but I needed her to know something. Looking into her eyes I told her "Yvette I'm sorry about the other night. I just got caught up in the moment and wanted you. I needed you".

She smiled and kissed me. "Baby don't apologize. It was good to see your wild side. I loved it." I smiled and kissed her then turned to walk away. I think that once I get my conversation with Jalyn out of the way life will be great. Right now I was headed home to sleep and sober up.

Chapter Ten

McKenzie

I was not expecting what came next. Cordell saw me and Steve arguing then walked over to us. This tall, dark, and handsome fellow grabbed Steve up and slammed him down. You saw the fear in this dude face. I wanted to laugh but I didn't know if I was next so I just stood back and watched.

Cordell threw a few punches to Steve's face then stepped back and looked at me. I won't lie. I was scared shitless. Then he looked back at Steve and said "If I ever catch you around my girl again I'm dropping you on sight".

He looked back at me again and this time he said "Baby are you ready to go? Lunch sounds better at my place anyway". I grabbed ahold of his arm and let him escort me out to my car. He didn't say a word until we got to my car.

Then he leaned into me, grabbed my face, and kissed me. "Now I see why you don't date and why you go hard on dudes when they come at you. But I'm not here for drama so we will handle him so that we can have a fulfilling relationship."

I kissed him again. He opened my car door and told me to follow him. We made it to his house and like he said we would we had lunch. He cooked! I had found a man that enjoyed cooking. Yesss!!! Cordell was turning out to be great.

"So Mr. James what are you looking for from me?" Sitting back at the kitchen table he just stared at me before speaking. "I see that you're a strong and independent woman." I interjected, "You don't know the half of that story".

He said "See that's what I'm talking about. I'm not trying to break you but I want you to trust again. I want you to trust me. Shit you have to trust me or we don't even have a shot". He was right and turning me on. "Look ain't no crazy ex gone run me away but anything less of a woman will."

Damn! I couldn't help it. I got up and walked over to him, put my right hand on his face, and straddled that man. Right there in his kitchen chair. I lowered myself onto his lap and fed that man my tongue. His tongue was thick and his mouth was inviting.

His fingers walked up my thighs and gripped my ass then around to my wetness. I began to moan between kisses. That must have driven him insane to hear me moaning in his ear. He stood up with me in his arms and carried me to the couch.

Cordell slowly undressed me. This man started with my feet and licked all the way up. When he reached that pot of gold waiting for him I lost all control. He removed his shirt and dove right in. It's like his tongue was a figure skater and my pussy was the ice rink.

Licking me up and down. Going in circles. Just driving me crazy! Then he started gently sucking on my pearl and drinking my juices causing me to grab his head and bury his face. I rode that wave and tried to drown that man but he was damn good. When he rose above me I couldn't help but sit up to meet his face and lick it.

Yeah I'm a freak. His face was covered in my juices and it looked good like that. Plus I wanted him to know that I was thankful for the multiple orgasms he had just given me. Cordell got completely undressed and I was immediately drawn to his manhood. He was fucking hung! I said before I knew it "Damn baby don't hurt me".

He laughed and told me "Baby around here pain is pleasure". As we kissed again he laid on top of me and inserted his huge dick inside of me. Ooh, he had me moaning so much and coming even more. This man was so thick and long that every stroke felt like insertion for the first time.

I was in heaven. When he took a pause I used it to my advantage. I pushed him back so that he was now seated and I straddled him once more but this time I meant business. Grabbing the back of his head I kissed his neck then back to his lips all while rocking my hips on his dick.

We kept going until he said "Shit baby you got me ready to bust already". That was my cue to jump off. I got off of his lap and onto my knees where I started to give him some superb head. He was going crazy. Thrusting his dick in and out of my mouth.

Faster. Harder. Until finally he pulled out and exploded all over my breast. He sat there drained. His breathing was shallow while I climbed up onto the couch smiling and satisfied. He reached out for me and pulled me close to him. We spent a while cuddling, kissing, and talking before heading off to shower together.

I hope this was the start to a meaningful relationship.

Chapter Eleven

Cordell

Damn. I figured she would be a great fuck but I didn't think she would get down like that. I had plans on making her mine but now I was definitely not letting her ass go. She was short, with full lips, thick hips, a fat ass, and long red hair. But more importantly it was her personality that shinned bright.

Even though she had a stalking ex-boyfriend I was here to stay. Fuck that frog looking muthafucka. She needed me to stick around whether she knew it or not. All independent women needed a man even if it was just for a good fuck.

This was going to be great. I just had to be careful how I played my cards with her. I had been following her on social media for a while and I knew that she was short tempered. McKenzie was already asking a million questions like we were getting married.

I needed to reassure her that life with me was where she was supposed to be. But first I'm going to leave this everlasting impression on her. So I jumped in the shower with McKenzie and teased her a little bit more. She couldn't take it and came in the shower all over my hand.

"This was definitely not what I had in mind for today but thank you."

"No need to thank me lil lady. I'm just doing my job." And with that statement I bent down and kissed her neck. She shivered and started blushing. This was going to be a piece of cake.

After the shower I asked her if she wanted dessert. Then I proceeded to the kitchen to whip up some cupcakes and further capture her heart. At first she laughed at the sight of me mixing up the batter.

"What a brother can't bake? I'll have you know that I don't just bake but I'm cold with my frosting too. Multi colored aka unicorn cupcakes are my favorite but I make a mean triple chocolate cherry cupcake or cake."

She was speechless. McKenzie shook her head then asked "Why are unicorn cupcakes your favorite? You don't have any children or do you?"

I put my first batch of cupcakes in the oven then turned to face her. I said with a slight smirk on my face "No but I'd like a few one day." Then I walked up to her and gave her a kiss.

I knew that everything that happened today was mind-blowing for her and I had no intentions on letting up. McKenzie told me about her life and her goals as we waited for the cupcakes to finish baking.

Since I knew that I had something up my sleeves and we were still in the kitchen I asked her to help me frost the cupcakes. Of course her answer was no but I made her come around.

I gave her step by step instructions on what to do. We had fun just experimenting with the food coloring before I showed her how to use a piping bag to ice the cupcakes.

No doubt I was winning right now. She said to me "I can't believe that I have no kids and I'm on a date yet I'm having a ball baking and icing cupcakes." This was great. I mean to see her beautiful smile was truly amazing.

Now that I had wowed her in some more untraditional ways I told her to go relax while I cleaned the kitchen. I showed her to my bedroom and helped her get comfortable then I returned to the kitchen.

I loaded my dishwasher and began cleaning up the small mess that we had made while having fun. As I was gathering the trash to take it out for pickup I noticed a familiar car parked outside.

Just as I exited my door she popped out of the car. "Hi baby! You miss me"?

Damn. Damn. Damn. It was my girl, Alese.

I hugged her and said "Hey baby. Don't I always miss you and daddy's baby"?

By now I was rubbing her stomach and talking to her stomach but as much as I wanted to keep this going I had to get her to go home. "Baby I wish you would have called me before just showing up. You know I hate when you pop up."

"I know but I was in the area and wanted to see you my love."

Wrapping my arms around her I told her "So why don't we do it this way. You go home and rest up because I got a few errands that I was about to run and when I'm finished I'm all yours."

She was smiling from ear to ear. But it worked. Alese got back in her car and blew me a kiss. "Don't keep me waiting baby!" Now I can get back to McKenzie who was laid up in my bed.

All that I could do was shake my head and keep it moving. I would have to lay down some rules so that I don't get caught up because I'll be damned if I put in all of this hard work for nothing.

Chapter Twelve

Jalyn

When I saw Matt standing over a feast fit for a King and Queen I knew that he was serious. I walked over to him and gave him a gentle kiss before having a seat. This time Matt was the aggressor and fed me his tongue while gripping my ass.

While I was shocked I was also loving the hell out of it. I loved a take charge man. He was making me want him more and more. Matt pulled out my chair for me like the gentleman that he is then he prepared a plate for me.

Everything looked so great yet nothing was too heavy of a food because we had work to do. Nothing was said but no words were needed. We both knew what we wanted and what was about to happen.

As we finished up our lunch Matt got up and pulled out my chair. I stood and followed him while he held my hand and led me down the hall to another room. The room was beautiful.

An oversized bed sat in the middle of the room with mirrors surrounding the room. I mean the walls were actually mirrors. The floor was covered in plush white carpet and on the other side of the room was a chase and fireplace.

I was in awe with this room. It was like a winter wonderland because the white décor bounced off of the mirrors and made the room so bright. Matt interrupted my thoughts by walking me to the bed and sitting me up on it.

He stood in front of me and began to undress me. Same as last time. Starting with my shoes then working his way up. Once my dress came off he dropped to his knees and began admiring my body.

I spread my legs and rubbed between my legs then stuck my fingers in my mouth. He was still on his knees but had started removing his clothes. As I started sucking on my fingers he followed suit and started stroking his dick. I smiled then watched him walk to me on his knees.

As I looked down at him kissing my feet and working his way up I went back to playing in my wetness. This time after I removed my fingers I put them in Matt's mouth. He licked and sucked my juices off of my hands in such a tantalizing way. He was already driving me crazy.

Matt pulled me to the edge of the bed in that same aggressive manner from earlier and I instantly got wetter. After I was where he wanted me he kissed my lips then dove right in. He had his arms around my legs locking me in place while he licked and sucked on my clitoris.

It was driving me crazy with each lick. Then he started rubbing and licking on my ass. Oh my goodness! This man was so skilled. I opened up for him without hesitation. Matt kept licking on my pussy while easing his finger in my ass.

It didn't take long before I squirted all over his face. That didn't stop him. I had to grab this man by his hair and pull him up to me. He fed me his tongue and I savored my flavor on his tongue.

As we were invading each other's mouth I slid down the bed and was now on my knees in front of Matt. He threw his head back and let out a grunt as I slid my mouth down the shaft of his throbbing dick.

I continued to wet his dick with my mouth then licked it all off. Licking all the way down to his testis then back up. I took him in my mouth until I began to choke. And let me tell you that he was well hung for a white guy.

He seemed to be losing control as I sucked his dick and played with his testis. Next thing I knew Matt had bent down and picked me up and inserted me leaving the condom on the floor unopened.

Realizing this I wanted to stop but I couldn't. It was too good to stop. I closed my eyes and got lost in the motion. Matt was holding me and bouncing me on his dick. I had never been done like this before.

He was blowing my mind and I was loving it. He turned and sat on the chase that was on the other side of the room. Now it was my turn to surprise him with my skills.

I wanted him to have all of me so I removed the teddy that I was wearing and let him admire my breast. That was all that he needed. He wrapped his arms around me bringing me closer to him so that he could suck on my nipples while I rode his dick.

His breathing quickened and so did mine. Each time I bounced up and down I felt like I was going to burst. Then I heard him moan and tell me how good I felt. I lost it. I came so hard that it made Matt climax too.

We just held each other until our breathing regulated. Matt started laughing as he hugged me. I laughed too because I already knew what was on his mind. The mind blowing sex that we had just had took both of us by shock.

But I'm glad that I shared this moment and my body with him and not some random guy. Matt ran me a bath with candles and actually bathed me. He was treating me like a Queen and I was loving it.

I guess maybe too much because now I didn't want to leave his side. At least not right now. That turned out to not be a problem though because when I got out of the tub he didn't want me jumping into the cold air.

Instead of me leaving, Matt ordered a movie and we snuggled in front of the fireplace watching our movie and finishing our dinner. Was this the start of something good or just a good encounter with a very nice and handsome man?

Chapter Thirteen

Malik

Some time had passed since I had purchased the ring and I was starting to get anxious about having it in my possession. I was wondering if I should go ahead and get it done.

I thought about it for a week straight and decided now was the perfect time to do it. I wasn't having any issues at work. There had been no communication between me and Jalyn so I wasn't as conflicted.

The most important thing was that me and my gal were on good terms too. I planned out all of the details because I wanted it to be a surprise that she would never forget.

The hard part was going to be getting in touch with all of her ratchet ass friends without them telling her or thinking that I was trying to fuck them. Nonetheless I was going to have to find a way to get at least her closest friends invited.

After thinking for a minute and finalizing the guest list I came up with a fool proof plan to invite her friends. I had my boys inbox her friends and made sure to express the need to keep their mouths shut.

That way I was done with that and could move on to the actual party planning. I wanted a place where we could really party. I wanted the eating, drinking, dancing, and pictures to all be on point.

I took a few days to look at some places before deciding on one. I decided to rent out the banquet room of a hotel that way I knew that we had enough space. Plus everything could be catered by the hotel itself. It was perfect.

My big sister wanted to be a part of the entire process so she made the invitations for me and sent them out with very clear instructions to not share on social media. Hopefully everyone read that part.

As the days passed I was a nervous wreck. I literally did a count down until the party. The night of the party Yvette had no clue what was happening. I had actually told her that we were just staying the night at a hotel for fun.

When we got there everyone was already in place so it was go time. We walked up to the door and when I opened it and she saw everyone she was in shock. Naturally she cried because she's just an emotional person. But when she saw the wall in front of her she cried even more.

On the wall was the big question spelled out in gold wedding bands, *Yvette will you marry me?*, along with our pictures playing in a slide on either side of the room. That's when I got down on my knee and asked her for her hand in marriage.

"Yvette you mean the world to me and there is nothing more that I would love than to make you Mrs. Jolten. Yvette my love will you marry me?"

Everyone waited for her response and once she managed to say yes through her sobs everyone screamed congrats at us. After we shared our moment and she began to mingle with the others she noticed that everyone was wearing custom shirts.

I had our closest friends wearing shirts that read, *Jolten Wedding coming soon!*, with wedding bells behind it. She said to me "You did all of this by yourself? I can't believe it.

You really love me." And then she started crying all over again.

Now that I had that out of the way I was feeling pretty good about life. I went on to bigger and better things at work because life had been so relaxing. Who knew that so much could change when you just went with the flow?

I had even stayed away from all social media for a while. I actually deactivated my accounts and was cool with it. Only reason I came back was to share the good news with the world. But I should have left it that way too because I didn't like what I saw when I came back.

Of course everyone took notice to me being back on the book when they saw the pictures of the party circulating. They congratulated me and her for days. But my happiness was short lived when I noticed Jalyn post something. It wasn't directed to me, I didn't think, but I needed clarity.

Again I should have stopped because what I saw on her page hit me like a ton of bricks. It didn't say that she was in a relationship but it was clear that she was.

There were so many pictures of her and her boss but they were anything but work pictures. They were out on dates, in the car together, he was driving her car which is a shock, and the most shocking one was of them in bed together having movie night.

My heart sank but I wasn't sure why. I had proposed to the love of my life so why was this an issue for me? I guess it was a reason why we stayed away from each other. Even though back then I thought it was good to talk things out with her I hadn't done it.

I guess that was a mistake. Now I didn't know how to even talk to my friend or if I should. I texted Jalyn and asked her if she wanted to meet up. She replied with much enthusiasm and said yes.

Regardless of my feeling about her I wanted my friend in my life no matter what. I was going to find a way to keep her around and still be happy at home. It was time that I let the new me take control. The me that somehow managed to change everything and was now living his best life.

Chapter Fourteen

McKenzie

This man was full of surprises. First he beats down my ex, gives me the bomb ass sex, then he bakes for me, and now we were on the road for a weekend trip. I couldn't get enough of this man although this little voice was telling me not to get attached.

Our first date had gone so well and we had been bonding over everything lately so he suggested that we take a romantic getaway. Of course I was all for it. Cordell had been nothing but good to me.

"Hey baby, are you ready for our getaway?"

I was wearing a huge smile but managed to respond "Yes baby. I've been ready. So where to?"

Cordell pulled out of my driveway and laughed saying "Can I surprise you just once"?

I sat back for a moment but that little voice told me to speak up. I said "Yeah baby but when you plan on taking me out of the state and out of my comfort zone then I'm a little curious".

It was things like this that made me a little uneasy. Cordell had this sneaky and mysterious side to him. I was going to need to have a girls night to get all the help that I could with this one. Jalyn definitely had the resources.

Just then I heard him say "Are you even listening to me? You asked me where we were going and then don't even listen to me when I tell you where we're going. Are you okay?"

"Yeah I'm good. Just had a thought cross my mind that's all."

After I said that we rode to the airport in silence. It's like he had something on his mind too. I didn't want to ruin what we had with silly accusations so I would definitely be calling Jalyn when we touched down.

For now I was going to enjoy this trip and hope that it wouldn't be our last one. Cordell finally spoke "Baby I'm sorry. I guess me wanting you to trust me went too far. You do deserve to feel comfortable. I'm sorry".

I was so relieved to hear him apologize. "I do trust you Cordell but you have to understand that we have only been together for a few months. Wait...are we even together? I just need for you to understand that just because I'm independent doesn't mean that you are not the man around here."

"So what I say goes?"

I gave him a crazy look before answering. "I mean for the most part, yes."

He smiled and kissed my hand. "For the record you are mine. I just like privacy but obviously I don't mind flaunting my baby around or we wouldn't be taking this trip."

That made my day. To hear him call me his baby in that way had me ready to pull over and get the party started right here on the side of the road. We made it to the airport and that's when I found out where we were going.

After going through so much security and being touched by all the wrong people I finally paid attention to our destination.

"Florida! You're taking me to Miami and didn't tell me!" I was livid with him right now yet happy too. Although I was mostly happy I wanted to be mad at him for not letting me know beforehand so that I could get myself together.

Even though I was already pretty fly I wanted to look extra fly heading to Miami. He said "Calm down ma I got that together already. Besides you look pretty damn good to me already". Cordell was licking his lips and making forget the anger I had built towards him.

I moved closer to him and kissed him on his neck. "You know that shit drives me crazy. You must be trying to miss this flight." I arched my back so that my breast and ass stuck out for him to see then nodded towards the restroom.

It would have gone down too if they hadn't called our flight. Now that it was time to go and I knew where I was going I texted Jalyn. I told her where I was headed and that we needed to link up once I touched back down.

She agreed and wished me luck on my flight and said to have fun with Cordell. I told her to have fun with Matt but not too much fun. I put my phone away and turned my attention back to the handsome man waiting for me at the gate.

This trip was going to be one for the record book. For one I had never been to Miami and two I was going with my man. That sounded great. I was happy that life had been going so well ever since Steve left.

Cordell must have really scared him because he just dropped off the face of the earth. No one knew what happened to that boy but I was happy to be drama free for a change.

I was living my best life and finally saving money like I wanted to. I had even given thought to marriage and kids one day, not any time soon though. Right now I was going to really enjoy spending time with Cordell and getting to know him better.

Chapter Fifteen

Jalyn

It had been a while since I heard from Malik and I was happy to hear from my friend. This was nothing new with us to disappear then come back and form an even stronger bond. I kind of loved that about our friendship. It kept it fresh because we always had catching up to do.

He texted me asking to meet up and of course I said yes. It was shocking that I hadn't heard from him sooner over the pictures Matt had been posting online. We weren't dating but it was nice to have someone to snuggle up to at night sometimes.

Then I got a text from Mac saying that she was going to Florida with her new man. Seems like life was okay for all of us. I was truly happy for everyone. Well everyone except Matt.

He was happy but ever since he started posting pictures of me and him his life was spinning out of control. All of these barbies started throwing themselves at him and telling him that he deserved better.

I wasn't mad but I wanted to end it so that he could find a woman that was all his because he and I were only friends with benefits. Matt didn't want to end it. He said that none of them would get his time because of their blatant disrespect.

Matt said "Any woman that can confess her feelings for me because of another woman having my attention is a gold digger and not worthy of me. Then to compare love based on color is utterly indignant behavior".

He was right. I wanted him to find love but not with anyone with hate in their heart because he saw no color. I loved and appreciate that about him. These women were going to have to do better if they wanted to get rid of me.

I met up with Matt for breakfast but it was work related. The office was waiting for us to mix the two but that only happened after hours when we had sex there. Other than that it was business as usual.

"Morning Suga"

"Good morning Boss"

He laughed. "We're not even at the office and you're calling me boss."

"Hey business is business no matter where it's been conducted."

Matt said "True. Which is why I wanted to meet with you. You've done well at the firm and are a huge asset to the company but how would you feel if one of us had to go"?

My eyes got huge. I was confused. "Am I being let go? Does it have anything to do with our "relationship"?"

"Calm down Suga no one is being let go. I simply asked how you would feel if one of us left the firm. That doesn't mean termination."

I felt slightly relieved but he needed to start talking and not in damn circles. I said "I don't know. I mean I've always wanted my own firm but I'm nowhere near that dream yet. Why? What's behind the questions and this meeting?"

Matt showed me a bank statement and said "Your dream is not a problem if you really want it." I was staring at the amount so hard that I missed the part that showed the account holders name. This was his personal account.

"Matt why are you showing me this? I like you for you not your money or what you can do for me. And why are you insisting that I leave Meebles?"

"Spending all of this time together has opened my eyes to see how you move in day to day scenarios. You are always on your toes and networking with people. You promote the firm hard and I just want you to put your all into your dream."

"But why now? I've always done that. I always give my all with whatever I do."

He looked at me with a smirk on his face and said "I know". I sat back and handed him back his bank statement. I was ready to go and was feeling like I had made a mistake crossing the line with him.

Matt said "Look I like your work ethics and I want you to have your own firm. No one has said anything about terminating either of us. I just want you appreciated because you're damn good at what you do."

He lowered his head and continued "And I want to give you something other than a nut and a good night's sleep." Now he was staring at me "We can be partners or you can own the business flat out. I can be a silent partner in the business but I'm ready for a change and you deserve one too."

So much was going through my head but I must admit that what he said was true. No one respected me at the firm even though I busted my ass doing work for my clients and to represent the firm.

We continued ordering breakfast while I pondered Matt's offer. Would I be making a wise choice opening a business with a man that I'm sleeping with? Was I ready to run a business myself? Was Matt serious or was there something else behind this?

I had so many questions. I needed a drink and some girl talk. I couldn't wait for McKenzie to touch down.

Chapter Sixteen

Malik

I spent the next few days picking out styles for my wedding so that as time passed I could just relax and wait. Yvette was thrilled and wouldn't stop talking about wedding stuff. She had been watching every show about marriage too.

It felt good watching her light up thinking of spending her life with me. Hell everybody wants to feel loved and wanted so I was eating this up. But I couldn't help but wonder why I still hadn't heard congrats from one person.

Jalyn still hadn't mentioned anything about me marrying Yvette. I know that she didn't care for her but I thought she would have at least humored me by saying it. Guess I was wrong.

Today I was meeting up with Arman to discuss more stuff about the wedding. It was just us two so the guy talk was unlimited. "Man I can't believe that you're taking that plunge."

I told him "Bruh we been together for hellas so why not". He nodded and we continued looking at venues since it was my task to find a place. Then he said "So what happened with Jalyn? You never told me what happened after y'all talked".

"I never got to talk to her. Life got busy and I just let it go. I saw on the book that she's dating her boss." I pulled up my account and showed him her page. He sat back and shook his head. He handed me back my phone and said "Damn homie looks like you locking down the wrong one".

I'm not sure what he meant but I had an idea hit me. I was going to tell her a few things that were on my mind and whatever happened next was meant to happen. But I had to stick to my guns this time.

I texted Jalyn and asked could we skip the meet up next week and talk tonight. I didn't care if she had plans with him. She said sure. I told Arman my plans and he was on board.

"Now you're talking my brother. Fuck the nice guy shit. Lay down law and let life happen." Shaking his head he finished with "Jalyn too fucking sexy to let her go anywhere. You better get her before he put a ring on her finger".

Damn. I hadn't thought of that. Were they that serious? Would she consider marriage? The Jalyn I knew wouldn't but I was starting to think that I didn't know her like I thought.

Arman was a good friend but sometimes I questioned this dude mindset. He was a careless and sometimes heartless guy. I didn't know if this was good or bad thing but this time I was taking a page from his book.

We continued to talk and he gave me more advice on life. It was mainly on how to do destress with all of this wedding talk and planning. He suggested taking a trip to just getaway.

That was a great idea. He suggested someplace where we could spend the first day doing tourist attractions, the next day doing guy shit and women doing them, and then the last day doing couple shit. It was fool proof.

Feeling good about this plan I was more energized to find a venue and get this wedding planned even quicker so that we could hurry to the trip. I just had to pitch this to Yvette and hope that she was game for it.

After another hour of searching I found one that caught my eye. I showed it to Arman and he liked the setup too. I texted some photos to

Yvette before calling to book a tour of the place.

She took a minute to respond but I guess she had to research the place for herself because when she texted back you could tell that she was excited. It was in all caps and simply read "YASSSSS!"

My work was finally finished for now. The next portion of my to do list wasn't due to start for another two week and that was the picking out of a tuxedo. I looked fly no matter what but I wanted to outshine everybody but the bride.

I'm not conceited but I take pride in how I look. After wrapping up my time with Arman I went to Jalyn's office to see if she was available. Unfortunately she was out to lunch with her so called boss.

I told her that I needed to see her and to meet me at her house and that I was already there. I awaited a text back from her but it never came. Instead I saw her blue Q4 pull up behind me in her driveway twenty minutes later.

Now there was turning back. I got out of my car and so did she. She looked sad and confused but I came here on a mission so I ignored her expression. I looked at her then turned to walk towards her front door.

I used the spare key she had given me when she moved in and left the door open for her. I caught a glimpse of her out of the corner of my eye and she had stopped walking and was looking even more confused.

This definitely wasn't the way I moved but I needed to clear my head without any interruptions. I needed her to know that I was serious. She obviously got the point. Once she made it inside she ran and grabbed my arm.

I spun around and stared into her eyes. For a brief second I saw fear in her eyes and I actually loved it. I took advantage of that second. I took a step closer to her and she started walking backwards. Now was the perfect time to strike so I did.

Chapter Seventeen

McKenzie

My vacation with Cordell was so peaceful. I still couldn't believe that he had flown us to Miami just to get away and have some fun. Who does that?! He was proving to me that I was a part of his life and that this was serious.

I had longed for this type of relationship. One where I could be treated like a Queen. This was so picture perfect yet I still had a feeling that I needed to shake. I had been home for a couple of days but took time to get back to work before telling anyone.

Soon as I clocked out today I planned on calling my girl to get this girls night underway.

I just hope that she wasn't planning on spending time with her boo thang. We both had been so consumed with the dick that we hadn't sat down in person in a while.

The last few months had shown me a lot of things. Things like every good strong woman needs some arm candy to savor every now and again. Also life had shown me who my real friends were.

I had so called friends trying to destroy my relationship with Cordell with bad advice. Others wanted me to put myself in compromising situations that I wouldn't want him in under any circumstances.

They even tried to temp him by getting in his DM. Can you believe them? They tried to bait my man just to take away my happiness and for what? So that I can be the miserable one while they go on in life with Tom, Dick, Harry, and Larry. These hoes ain't loyal.

But Jalyn was real and that's why I couldn't wait for this work day to be over already. I needed the bottle of wine that I had waiting on me and some girl talk. I texted her because I couldn't wait until later to confirm her plans.

After a few minutes I texted her again. Still no response. This wasn't like her and I was starting to regret not calling her as soon as I got back in town. I looked on the book to see if she had been active. Nothing. I was spooked.

I gave it some time before taking a break and calling her phone. At first it just rang. This was good. Maybe she was on a case. I returned to work happy with the thought that she was actively in the field.

Since she was busy I went out to dinner with a few coworkers after work. The food was so on point that I almost forgot where I was and was about to kick off my shoes.

Everyone paid for a round of drinks whether we were still drinking or not. We were just there for the laughter. I had a good time hanging with them but now that I was full of food I wanted my bed.

I thanked my coworkers for a great night and jumped in my car to head home. I noticed that Cordell's house was on my way home so I decided to go by there to see if he was home.

I was pumped to see my man and maybe get some good dick tonight but I guess I should have stuck to my first plan to go home. As I approached his house I noticed that his car wasn't there but another one was parked in his driveway.

Who could've been there if he wasn't there? I called him just to see what he was up to and of course he answered my call.

"Hey beautiful, what's up?"

"Hey baby. What are you up to?"

"Not much baby. In bed already trying to rest for my trip in the morning."

I had forgotten about his business trip that he had. Maybe that would explain why he didn't have his car but some random car was in his driveway. I pulled off not wanting to disturb his rest.

"Well I would have loved to have seen you but I'll let you rest."

"Yeah baby you know I head out early. I'll make sure to touch down and come right to you."

I was all smiles as I drove away. That was until I saw his metallic Mercedes turn the corner heading for his house with a female driving. Who the fuck is this bitch?

I played things cool and told him that it sounded like a plan as I drove away. Now I knew why I had that gut feeling that something was off. I was trying not to be crushed just yet. I needed to dig a little deeper first.

Picking up my phone I dialed Jalyn praying that she would finally answer. Yes! She answered on the first ring. "Jalyn I need your help. I'm asking as a friend but if I have to pay you I will."

"No need for that just give me the details and get off the road because you sound very distraught."

"You don't know the half of it. I'm on my way to you now."

"Okay. I'll leave the door unlocked for you. I'll be in my office waiting."

I couldn't get to her house quick enough but I managed to safely arrive there. Now I was praying that what I had seen could be explained. Maybe he had a sister that I didn't know about. Maybe I was overreacting. Just maybe.

Chapter Eighteen

Jalyn

I didn't know what to think of Matt's offer. We continued to discuss details over breakfast and I started to see that he was genuinely trying to help me start my own firm.

"Matt I would only feel right being business partners if we were no longer sexual partners."

Matt lowered his eyes and sat silent for a moment. Then he looked at me and said "I respect your decision. Doesn't mean that I like it or want it. You mean a lot to me Jalyn."

I didn't want to hurt him but the thought of owning my own business or even being a partner with him was beginning to sound exciting the more I thought about it.

"Matt I would love to own my own firm but I would love to be your business partner even more. I want happiness for you also. So what do you say?"

"Why can't we have both?"

I had no idea that Matt had caught feelings for me like this. It was nice to feel wanted but I didn't want to mix business with pleasure. I liked Matt and could see happy times with him but were they long term?

Even if they were I still couldn't mix business with pleasure. Just then I looked down at my phone and noticed that I had a text from Malik that seemed urgent. What was going on with him lately?

Matt saw the expression on my face and asked "What's wrong? Did I come on too strong or overstep my boundaries? I didn't mean to."

I quickly shook my head and responded "No you are fine. It's just that I'm needed by a good friend of mine. Seems important."

"Oh I'm sorry. Do you need me to come with you?"

"No I should be fine. I'm just going to meet him there and see what's going on."

Matt looked confused for a second. He said "Him?" I sat up straight and looked him in his eyes and said "Yes, My friend Malik." That's when the expression on his face changed. He was relieved.

I said my goodbyes to Matt and headed to my car. Pulling out my phone I read the text again and decided not to respond but just show up. I needed to get to the bottom of whatever was bothering him.

As I pulled into my driveway I noticed that Malik was still at my house and parked in my way. I didn't even have a chance to tell him to move because he jumped out and gave me the dirtiest look.

I got out but thought twice about going in with him. Instead I was going to suggest staying outside but then he used the key I had given him years ago when I bought the house.

How stupid of me to forget that he had a key but why would he use it and I'm right here. His actions where making me feel some type of way. After he made entry into my house I ran to stop him.

Grabbing his arm in hopes that he would stop did nothing. He turned towards me with fire in his eyes. My mind was racing with reasons that would make him act this way.

Was he on drugs? He never did them before but this was unlike him so maybe he started. Then I thought maybe it was over me and

Matt. But what he didn't know was that we were just friends.

All sorts of things crossed my mind. I even had the thought of calling for help because he was tripping. As we stood face to face I saw a coldness inside of him. I started to back away.

Malik wouldn't let me get away. He started moving with me. I moved a little quicker and he did too. He smirked then he grabbed me up by my throat and held me against the wall.

I didn't know what to do. This was the same person that I had told I love you to. Tears wanted to form but I couldn't cry. Not now. Now I needed to figure out what was going on and my next move as well as his. Malik began asking me questions.

"Are you still fucking your boss?"

I was now mad and confused at the same time. "What? Is this what all of this is about? No, we ended it this morning."

His grip tightened around my throat and he said "Good. That shit is forever dead because you belong to me. That ass is mine. Do you understand?"

I couldn't believe what I had just heard. Jealousy was something that I never expected from Malik. It kind of turned me on. Now I knew what was going on. He had serious feelings for me too.

Although I had figured things out the fact still stood that this crazy muthafucka had me in a choke hold right now. My eyes searched his for a clue to his mindset but there was nothing. Darkness.

I finally answered him "Malik I've always been yours but you chose to give your heart to her." That's when he loosened his grip and his eyes softened. This was more of the man that I knew. But we were far from finished.

Chapter Nineteen

Malik

After I grabbed Jalyn up and held her against the wall I saw that fear that made me feel superior for some reason. I took that time to tell her that she was mine and she said that she was always mine.

Hearing her say that she was mine but I gave my heart to someone else hurt deep down. I loosened my grip on her throat and kissed her. That's all I could do. I wanted her. I needed her.

I knew that it was wrong because I was due to get married in a few months but Jalyn had my heart. Always had. I held her tight and kissed her deeply. She wrapped her legs around my waist and kissed me like no one ever had.

Her lips were so soft. Her touch was so gentle. Between her legs was getting moist. Her body was calling for me. I picked her up and led her to the dining room table. I laid her down and began to undress her.

I did what I do best and devoured her pussy like it was my last meal. I can never get enough of her when she cums over and over again. I absolutely loved that shit. But today was different because I wasn't going to stop with eating her pussy.

After she begged me to stop and had cum numerous times I undressed and she watched my every move. I stood and let her admire my body. Her hands caressed my chest and she let her fingers trace my tattoos. Then she grabbed me by head and kissed me.

As we kissed I slid into her wet and waiting pussy. She felt so good. There is no way that I could let her go back to him or anyone else. I played with her clitoris while I gave her long deep strokes causing her to have back to back orgasms.

The way she moaned had me ready to bust but I had to see what that mouth do first. I pulled out and stood back. She instantly knew what to do. Jalyn dropped to her knees and sucked all of her juices off of my dick.

Then she took all of me into her mouth and started deep throating me like crazy. She was slurping on me and playing with herself. She was driving me insane. Her body was so gorgeous.

I had only dreamed of taking Jalyn like this but to have her on her knees sucking on my dick was more than I could handle at the moment. I told her that I was about to cum and she sucked faster and harder. I fell in love the moment she swallowed my nut.

Jalyn kept sucking sending me into overdrive. I had never had a chick suck dick like her. Her mouth was just as wet as her pussy and it felt so damn good. I wasn't finished with her.

I picked her up and carried her to her bed then laid her down but she had other plans. She instructed me to lie back on the bed so I did as I was told. That woman mounted herself on my dick and took me for the ride of a lifetime.

The view was amazing. Watching her caramel skin glisten and her big breast bounce as she bounced on my dick was a dream come true. She was perfect. And her riding was superb but this was my show.

I flipped her back onto her back then gently choked her as I entered her and pushed her legs back by her head. Fuck she was flexible!

I fucked Jalyn and told her "This is my pussy and you belong to me. Don't ever take your love away from me."

Just like that she came all over my dick again and again screaming "Oh my gosh Malik I'm coming!" She couldn't stop and I was in heaven. As I hit her with that choke stroke and felt her gush I came again.

We both just laid there in awe for a minute before I repeated what I said to her a minute ago. "You belong to me and you will forever be mine. No one can or will stop that from being true."

She smiled and kissed me softly on my lips then my neck before stating "So make sure that you remain true to me."

I looked at her trying to figure out what she meant but it really didn't matter. She was the one that truly had my heart so I would do anything to protect her and make her happy.

After we talked for a while about our feelings for one another Jalyn got up to shower. "You want to join me?" I got up and hugged her bare body. This was the greatest feeling ever.

We entered the shower together and watching the water cascade over her body had me hard again. I played with her and sucked on the back of her neck while she moaned out loud from pleasure.

She came all over my hand then dropped to her knees in the shower and sucked one out of me again. After we had cum again we showered and headed back to the bed where we just laid and held each other.

Jalyn's phone had been going off all day yet she hadn't answered. This time when it went off she answered and told whoever it was to come by. I didn't know who it was yet I didn't want to ask either.

So I asked her "Shall I be leaving now?"

She said "No. Why would you be going anywhere? You're home now."

Chapter Twenty

McKenzie

When I got to Jalyn's house I noticed another car in her driveway but I didn't really care who it was at this point. I knew it wasn't Matt because he drove some fancy ass car that I couldn't afford.

I entered the house and headed for her office like she told me to. On the way down the hall I caught a glimpse into her bedroom. In her bed was this extra yellow inked up guy who I recognized as her friend Malik.

What was he doing here? So that's why she wasn't answering her phone. I made it back to her office and gave her the stare of death. She said "What? Why the serious face?"

"So you ignored all of my calls for some dick?" I teased

"Umm, I've had a long day and honestly didn't know who was calling or that my phone was even ringing."

"Damn. The dick is that good? So what about Matt?"

"Long story short we ended it this morning to be partners at our own firm."

My eyes lit up. "Are you serious? That's great news! I mean besides the part of you losing your boo. When you get details I want to know everything. I will be your first client." I started shaking my head.

"Okay so what's up with you needing a detail on someone? I thought you and Cordell were good. Spill the tea."

I began to tell her everything that happened since we've met. The great, the good, and the bad that had just occurred. She shook her head and I knew what was coming next so I beat her to it.

"Instead of jumping to conclusions and cursing his ass out I called you to do a little work for me. So what do you say? Will you help me?"

I nudged her arm and gave her sad big eyes. Jalyn laughed and turned to her computer to login. I was so excited to be one step closer to some answers. "Hey so I guess we're just going to ignore the fact that you got Mr. GQ in your bed."

She started laughing and said "Umm that's Malik. I thought you two met already."

"No and I don't care if we had met before. Why is he in your bed and it looked like he was half naked or fully. I wasn't trying to see all of that."

She turned to me and whispered "Yes he's been here most of the day fucking me like he's crazy. Forreal. I don't know who that muthafucka is but he look as good as Malik and he said I was his so he can stay."

We both burst out laughing. I really wished that they could be together because Jalyn loved him but I honestly didn't see that happening. Hell it took them over fifteen years to admit that they wanted each other.

Jalyn began running searches online to find possible family that maybe I didn't know about. We found out that he had a brother but no sister. Jalyn said "Maybe it was a cousin that was just visiting."

I wanted to believe that but my gut wouldn't allow me to. Next I asked her to do a little surveillance when he got back because I still felt like something was wrong. She agreed but said it was going to cost me.

I didn't like when she talked like that because she always wanted work done but I agreed. Jalyn asked me if we were friends on any social media sites and I said "Yes but he has no activity as far as I can see".

That was another red flag because it never dawned on me that we were and that he had told me not to tell the world our business. He always stressed his need for privacy.

I had her look into that and it seemed that was all of the investigating that we needed to do. This muthafucka was in a relationship and she was pregnant. How did I not know this? He hid it from my account?

As I got lost in my thoughts I got really quiet. Too quiet for Jalyn. She said "Do not do anything crazy. Give him a chance to explain everything."

I stood up and stormed out of the room yelling "What's there to explain? This asshole lied to me for six months. How the hell did I not realize it? Better yet how the hell did he do it?"

Jalyn nodded and continued "Now that's a better question. How was he able to keep you two away from each other and take trips like he's single? You've been to his home and stayed the night. Sorry but he's good."

I didn't want to admit it but he was good. Too good to let him leave thinking that he had everything under control. I said bye to Jalyn and stormed out of her house. I had a stop to make before heading home.

My mind was racing. Even though I knew that I shouldn't be doing this my mind was telling me that I'd be crazy not to do this. Jalyn knew that I was up to something because she wouldn't stop calling me but I had to do this solo.

I pulled up to Cordell's house and called him. No answer. Oh so he won't answer because she was there so I texted him instead.

Come outside before she finds out tonight!! Not even a minute later he was running to my car.

I unlocked the door and he got in then I drove off with him in the car.

Chapter Twenty One

Cordell

I couldn't believe that I had dodged that bullet with McKenzie. She didn't know that I had seen her pull up before she called me. The last thing that I needed was to be seen talking to her at my house. Shit I could play it off anywhere else but not home.

Just as I was putting my phone back on the charger I heard Alese walk back in the house. Shaking my head was all that I could do at that close call. I helped my baby get situated so that we could eat all that she could before her cutoff time.

Due to her having a cesarean tomorrow she couldn't eat after midnight so we were eating everything that she could think of. I watched her feed my baby and smiled knowing that I would be able to meet this little person soon.

After we ate I helped her bathe and relax because I knew that she was nervous. I was nervous. This was the first child for both of us so we had no clue what to expect.

When Alese got out of the bathtub I told her to let me do everything for her. I wanted her completely relaxed. I dried her off then oiled her up before putting her in the bed and getting in myself.

We hadn't been in bed watching television for a good half an hour when my phone rang. I'll be damned if it was Mac. I silenced it and of course a text came through. *Come outside before she finds out tonight!*

I told Alese that I needed to talk business and she didn't pay me no mind so I got up to go call her back but I noticed that this bitch was outside my house again. I ran outside before I knew it ready to fuck her up.

But once I opened her car door and got inside she drove off like a bat out of hell. "What the hell is your problem?! Why are you showing up at my spot and threatening my gal?"

I probably fucked up with that last statement because she slammed on breaks causing me to brace myself yet I still hit my head. She gave me a very dirty look and said "Your girl?"

Now that the car was idle I tried to get out but she locked the doors and peeled off in a hurry before I could get out. I was furious at this point. "McKenzie you got ten seconds to pull the fuck over before I beat yo ass."

Again she slammed on breaks and turned to look at me. "Bitch you don't have any right talking to me that way! You fucked up and now you have the audacity to be the one with an attitude? Fuck you!" She punched me in my head

Okay so maybe she was right. I should have played this different. "Mac you're right. My apologies."

She was pissed and my words fell on deaf ears right now. I really shouldn't be mad that she called me out or that she even knew about Alese. I tried again to change the mood. "Do you want to lead the conversation or should I?"

Mac drove in silence until we reached her house. I was relieved to see that she brought us here instead of someplace suspect. I valued my life which is why I was about to try and make up to Mac at whatever cost.

We walked inside and she flopped down on the couch. I came over and removed her shoes. Of course she fought the entire time until she just broke down crying and lost all of the will to fight.

Now was my time to take charge. I removed her pants and shirt just trying to get her comfortable. She continued to cry while I did this then she flipped out on me. She began swinging on me and throwing shit.

"Mac calm down and let me explain!"

"Explain what? You know my past and still chose to do me this way. What kind of "man" are you really? I should have known better."

She was now calm again and crying. I walked over to her and began to explain myself.

"Just listen. I never meant to hurt you. Yes I have a baby on the way but I want you. I know that sounds selfish but I found someone that I enjoy being around. Look at all the time that we spend together."

She was still silent so I continued "You mean a lot to me Mac and I'm not letting you walk away. You will continue to be my baby. I just have a baby on the way. She means something to me because of the gift that she's carrying but you have my heart. I love you McKenzie."

With those words she stopped crying and a blank expression was on her face. Then she said "If you love me then you'll end it with her or let me go but you won't do this to me."

"I understand but my heart won't let me do that. This isn't the time to break her down like that. But trust me when I say that you are mine and I am yours."

I moved closer to her and kissed her. She didn't pull away so I went for it. I parted her legs and dove in head first. After her first orgasm she had relaxed and gave in. I wasn't finished though. I was about to make another major move.

Normally we used protection but tonight I took her raw in this vulnerable state. It was the best feeling and there was no way that I was going back to protection. Besides there wouldn't be a need to because I made sure that I didn't pull out.

Chapter Twenty Two

Jalyn

I had been terrified when I saw Malik two weeks ago but it turned out to be a really good visit. Fuck that it was a great visit. He had come by and expressed his feelings for me in the most aggressive yet fulfilling way. Ever since then we had been hanging out and having fun.

Malik had really opened up to me about life and I loved his company. I had always fantasized about being with him and sexing him like he was mine but now I had him. I was on cloud nine.

At least I was until I caught myself lusting over him one day so I logged into the book to look at his pictures and one of his post blew me away. The caption read that the countdown was on and was accompanied by a ton of pictures of people wearing Jolten Wedding shirts.

My heart sank. Hell I thought that I was going to have a heart attack the way that it was beating right now. How the hell did I miss this? I read the date and realized that this all took place before he showed up at my house pouring out his heart to me.

I felt so betrayed. I called up my girl that I hadn't talked to since she ran out of my place over news that her guy was cheating too. Damn these dudes ain't shit. She answered immediately.

"Hey bestie, what's been going on with you?" She sounded so chipper

"Lies. All lies. Everything that he said to me was a lie. What's been up with you though?"

She laughed which was a little scary coming from her after that question. So I asked her "What happened with Cordell? Did you do something crazy?"

"Umm, he's still here. We need to talk about this over dinner tonight." Mac was laughing again but this time I was too. She was still with him after she got all mad about his baby momma. I couldn't wait for dinner.

I hadn't taken any new cases because Matt and I were in the process of getting a business loan together to officially start our own firm. It still felt weird to me that we were just lovers and we're now headed towards owning a firm together.

The thought of owning a company made me smile and call Matt. He answered with his usual "Hey Suga."

""Hey Boss"

"Now you know that you're going to need to change that title to partner right?"

"I can do that. So how is everything? Need anything from me?"

"You know now that you mention it I could use some lunch. I've been going through some paperwork and haven't eaten yet."

"Sure thing, partner."

I could tell that he was smiling as we ended our call. Matt still wanted a relationship and honestly I wish I would have given him a chance instead of Malik. Anyhow, since he wanted food that was the least that I could do for him.

I decided to go to the grocer instead of buying some take out. I was going to cook for Matt since he was taking care of all of the paperwork. It was the least that I could do. Of course I read it all over once he got it together then we signed everything together.

After leaving the grocer I headed to Matt's house to help in as many ways as I could. I arrived and he was happy to see me especially after he saw that I was prepared to cook.

"I've missed your cooking so much. You get tired of cooking when it's just you eating. After a while you're like what's the use."

"Well then let me get moving so that you can keep on grooving."

He laughed and went back to working and I made him a quick yet fulfilling dinner. I was so distracted with my thoughts about Malik that I hadn't noticed Matt come into the kitchen.

"What's troubling you Suga?"

I jumped and turned to say "Nothing just tired."

He laughed and said "You're a horrible liar."

I laughed and finished preparing dinner for my partner. When it was done Matt ate and just sat quietly watching me as I looked over the papers that needed signatures. Then he finally spoke.

"You know that I would never do you wrong in any way yet you still won't bite. What does he have that I don't?"

I didn't need to ask him who or how he knew anything. We are private investigators and I'm sure Matt made it his business to watch me. I didn't answer. I signed the necessary documents and gave him a kiss on the forehead before leaving.

But once I made it to my car the tears flowed ever so freely. What did Malik have that I couldn't get from Matt? I knew the answer but I couldn't tell Matt because Malik had my heart. All of my heart.

Chapter Twenty Three

Malik

These last two weeks had been great. I finally had my venue for my wedding along with most of the decorations in order and I had been getting all of the fellas together for their tuxedo fittings.

Things were moving along in the right direction. Jalyn and I had been seeing each other on a regular with no problems. I had the best of both worlds going on with Yvette and Jalyn.

After my morning meeting I noticed that I hadn't heard from Jalyn all day. That wasn't normal. We both were early risers and would communicate every morning and throughout the day.

I texted her a simple hey in hopes of hearing from my sexy lil secret but after a few hours I hadn't heard back from her so then I texted her again. This time I got a reply. It read "Congrats. And good luck on your nuptials."

I was hurt and angry that she had found out before I could tell her. True I've known for some time that I was getting married soon and I hadn't told her but this wasn't an easy task. She had my heart.

Not being able to focus I left work and headed straight to her house but she wasn't there. I texted her to come home but she refused. Next I tried my luck and called her.

"I really don't want to talk to you Malik."

"Hear me out Jalyn. I wanted to tell you but the timing was never right."

She yelled into the phone "That's because you were always fucking my brains out! You didn't think this little detail was important Malik?!"

I could tell that she had been crying. Her voice carried so much hurt in it and it was all my fault. This was a disaster. How could I calm her down and keep her?

"Baby I am truly sorry. I wanted to tell you. I never wanted you to find out from any other source."

"Bullshit! You put it on the fucking internet for everyone to see. So everything that you said to me was a lie?"

"No! It was the truth! I love you so much and I never want to lose you. We have so much history that I'm not willing to erase. Baby can we talk face to face?"

"All I am is a good fuck to you. You don't care about me. I hope that bitch can give you everything that I did because I'm over it. You are wrong for this. She'll never love you like I love you."

And with that she hung up on me. I can't lose her so what do I do? This hurt me and I couldn't bring myself to go home with this on my mind and heart.

I decided to go into Jalyn's house and wait for her. This had become normal for us. Me cooking or her cooking while the other cleans. It felt right on so many levels that it made going home hard every time.

Yvette called me while I was there but I sent her to voicemail. She thought that I was at work anyway so I didn't have to answer her right now. I never thought that this would blow up in my face like this.

Just as I was sitting everything on the dining room table for Jalyn's arrival she walked in and slammed the door.

"You don't belong here. Get the fuck out of my house!"

"No. We have to talk Jalyn. I'm not letting you go and I'm not going anywhere. I love you."

Her shoulders slumped and her head was low. She said "I know you do. I can tell that by the way you treat me, talk to me, and the time that you put into everything that we do."

I smiled and walked up to her for a hug. She didn't object. Instead she started crying in my arms. I fucked up and felt horrible about it. This was by far one of the worst moments that I had ever gone though.

"I understand if you no longer want to talk to me but I really don't want you to walk out of my life."

"So why are you marrying her? You're not really mine."

"Jalyn I'll always be yours. You're mine and I'll spend as much time as I need to making you understand that."

We both looked into each other's eyes and just like that the fight was over. Although she didn't have an appetite she thanked me for the dinner and we spent the rest of the afternoon in bed.

I made Jalyn a promise that I would take care of her and I plan to keep it regardless of my soon to be marriage. What Yvette didn't know wouldn't hurt her. For some reason I needed them both and would do anything to keep it that way.

Now that Jalyn was taken care of it was time to go home and be the best fiancé that I could be.

Chapter Twenty Four

McKenzie

I had lost all feeling in my body when he touched me. We had made love and it felt so damn good. It was like nothing that I had ever felt before. For the first time in my life I was in love.

Not just with the sex but with the man. I had never been in a relationship where a man cared about me and would do anything to prove it to me. Yeah dudes do dumb shit and think that it's love but I felt it when Cordell said it.

I needed this man around. I didn't care that he had had a baby or that she still wanted him. That was my man and no one was going to change that fact. No one.

Jalyn called me sounding distraught so I told her that dinner was on me. We had to catch up anyway because I missed my friend. Dealing with these nutty ass dudes had time flying by.

When I pulled up to The Best Damn Mexican restaurant I noticed that Jalyn was already inside. It was just like her to arrive early no matter where we were going. That was just her style.

I walked inside and saw her already seated with two huge margaritas at the table. She had already started on hers. I laughed when I saw it and she waved at me then motioned toward the second margarita.

"Hey girl, I see you got started without me this time."

"Yeah I had to this time. So how was your day?"

"Girl it was a day. Same dumb shit at work but what's up with you? What's going on?"

"Well when I called you I had just found out that Malik proposed to that bitch. They're getting married in four months. Can you believe that?"

I couldn't believe what I was hearing and had actually spit out some of my margarita.

"Hell to the nah! He's fucking nuts. When did he tell you this?"

"That's just it Mac he didn't tell me. I just happened to be on his page and saw the news. Two weeks ago he proposed AND professed his feelings for me."

My friend was fucked up. It showed all in her face. I won't lie I was genuinely shocked by this news because I never thought that

Malik had it in him. He was a square in my book compared to some her ex boo thangs.

"Wow so how are you holding up?"

She laughed and said "I guess I'm a fool in love because after I called you I went to see Matt. Business only but then Malik called me. I hung up on him not wanting to talk but when I got home I found him in my house cooking me dinner for tonight. So we ended up talking then having sex before I ended up here drinking my sorrows away."

"Damn. We truly are some loyal ass hefas." We both started laughing then she asked "So I take it everything is okay between you and Cordell?"

Again we laughed. See we had been friends for so long that we knew shit before the other one even said anything. Our friendship was something special that most people wouldn't understand.

We never judged each other but were always there for on another no matter what. I looked at her and still saw sadness in her eyes so I gathered my thoughts and let the words flow.

"Girl so what that man is getting married. Y'all have been friends for so long that nothing or no one should get in the way of that and if he really cared about that woman then he wouldn't be doing this in the first place."

She nodded so I continued "He loves you and you love him. Anyone with eyes can see that. Hell Ray Charles could see that. So if your heart wants to be with that man then enjoy the ride until it ends. Just let it end on your terms. Fuck him."

By now she was feeling better. Sitting up and looking happier she asked me "Is that what you said about your boo?"

"Oh I damn near killed that bitch but yeah he's not going anywhere. I'm happy and he will continue to deliver happiness to me until I see fit."

I told her everything that happened that night and everything after that day. We had good laughs over our fucked up love lives but deep down we knew that they were fucked up.

But who wants to be bored and lonely all of the time? Not me so I will have my fun while I can and wait for my Mr. Right. That's why I told Jalyn to do the same. She explained to me that Matt still wanted her but that her heart was in it with Malik.

As a friend I had to tell her to follow her heart. I just hope that she didn't get hurt. Nor did I want to get hurt either. We sipped on more margaritas and laughed over more dumb shit in our lives like work and family.

It was great to express my feelings and not be called dumb or stupid for loving someone that loved me. She was in the same boat so she felt my pain. All of this talking about men while drinking was making me want Cordell right now so I texted him. *Bring it to me. Now*!

Chapter Twenty Five

Cordell

I was happy that me and McKenzie was doing good but she was killing me with the sex. It was like she couldn't get enough of it. I was hoping that this meant that she was pregnant because I wanted her ass to give me a child soon.

Mac didn't want children but I saw great mother skills in her and I wish she had just given birth not Alese. Don't get me wrong Alese was a cool girlfriend at the time but she wasn't ready for motherhood. It just happened.

I had just put the baby down for a nap when my phone went off. It was Mac saying that she wanted the dick right now. Everything in me wanted to dick her down but I was on the other side of town with my baby.

I texted her back saying that I would see her tomorrow and make it up to her. She didn't respond which meant she didn't like my response. To get a reaction out of her I went into the bathroom and sent her a dick pic.

It worked too. She returned the favor making it hard for me to concentrate on Alese. This was becoming hard because I liked Alese but I was falling in love with Mac. It was something about her that I was drawn to.

Something had to happen quick because I didn't know how much longer I could keep doing this dance with the two of them. I wasn't big on broken homes but like I said getting Alese pregnant was an accident.

Alese walked into the bedroom wearing a red lace bra and panty set trying to seduce me. That was not lingerie in my book nor was she turning me on. I was losing my interest but I had to fake it until the time was right.

"The baby is asleep so I figured we could work on us. You know, spend a little time together."

"Alese it's only been two weeks since you had the baby. We can't do anything yet."

She pouted and looked like I hurt her feelings. Fuck! I just couldn't win but there was no way that I was going in that soon. "But I'm not bleeding anymore and I feel fine."

I shook my head and said "No ma'am. I cannot and will not."

She said "Well maybe I can do something for you."

Next thing I knew she was on her knees pulling my dick out. I would've stopped her but I didn't need the argument so I did my best to help her out. As she put me in her mouth I started to get hard but who wouldn't.

My mind drifted off to thoughts of McKenzie. She had me gone in the head and I wasn't the one to fall in love easily. I started fantasizing about Mac's head game while Alese was working her mouth.

Next thing I knew I was moaning out loud and fucked up. I mumbled "Damn Mac your mouth feels so good."

I didn't realize what I said because Alese didn't stop. So my thoughts kept going. "Yeah baby let daddy nut in your mouth. Swallow this shit." That's what caught her attention.

She jumped back as my dick jerked and I began to bust. "Um, who is Mac and since when do I swallow? Please explain."

"Really Alese? You just gave me the best blowjob and you start trippin immediately." I got up shaking my head and heading towards the bathroom to get clean even though I was the one trippin.

She followed me to the bathroom still questioning me. So who is she? I turned towards her and grabbed her by the waist pulling her to me. "Baby you were doing such a good job I called you a mac. There is no one else."

I kissed her forehead and saw a smile on her face but it slowly faded. Alese said "But I've never swallowed before and you said that shit like I was a pro at drinking nut."

Again I kissed her but this time on her lips and told her "It's a first time for everything. I just figured I'd try today."

I could tell that I had made her feel guilty for not attempting to swallow. Shit I was just happy that she fell for what I was saying to her when I was the one fucking up.

Alese kissed me and apologized before slowly walking away. Normally I would have chased after her and made her feel better but I had Mac on my mind. Looks like I was on my way to her after all.

Looking at my watch I noticed that it was a little after eleven by the time I had finished getting dressed and leaving for Mac's house. I figured that she would be awake because she was a mover and shaker like me.

I was right too. As I approached the door I could hear music softly playing in one of the back rooms. I knocked and she appeared a few seconds later looking good as ever.

No words were said as I walked in and wrapped her in my arms. She wrapped hers around me and we went in at the front door. I don't know what it is about this one but she had a hold on me.

I was hypnotized looking into her eyes as I raised her up and lowered her onto my dick.

At that moment I realized what I had to do to get my life where I wanted it. But that would have to wait until after this nut.

Chapter Twenty Six

Jalyn

Walking into my house and seeing Malik was not what I wanted but after my breakdown in Matt's driveway and Mac's words buzzing in my head I didn't put up much of a fight.

I knew that he would never be mine but after fifteen years of fantasizing about him what did I have to lose. I didn't want to lose my friend and I was spoiled to the way that he showed me attention and his company.

So Malik and I talked for a while before making our way to bed. He had been at my house cooking dinner for me while I was out.

It was a sweet thought but I was in no mood to eat.

We lay in bed talking over our arrangement and kissing like crazy. A little sex. But it was something about his lips that I couldn't resist. I had to kiss him constantly. Every other word was followed by a kiss.

He didn't seem to mind. In fact he loved it. But I had to be honest with him about my feelings before he left. "Malik I hate how you did me and everything in me hurts right now but I just can't let you go."

He started to interrupt but I silenced him and continued. "She is nothing more than a gold digger waiting to benefit however she can from all of your hustle. Please do not cry to me when she fucks you over."

His face was priceless. Yes he knows that I keep it very honest but I think that was unexpected coming from me. At this point he would see a lot more of that brutal honesty if he planned on playing with my heart.

Just as Malik and I were finishing up our conversation I got a text from a number that I didn't recognize. It read *Hey baby. How are you? Can we talk?* So I replied, *Who are you trying to reach?*

After I walked Malik to the door I returned to find my phone ringing. I noticed that it was the number that had texted me a minute ago. I answered it out of curiosity. "Hello"

"Hey beautiful, how have you been? Long time no talk." As the caller spoke I heard a familiar voice on the line.

"Well hey there Trei. I'm good but how have you been?"

"I'm good baby. I miss you. Can we meet up?"

"Sure can! Stop by anytime I'm still in Florissant. I miss you too."

"Great. I'll see you soon."

Oh my goodness that was an unexpected call but a welcomed change in the usual faces in my life. It was a call from my ex LaTrei with his sexy ass. This man was tall with the sexiest hazel eyes, caramel skin like mine, and a sexy ass body with tattoos all over. You can tell that this man worked out.

I hadn't seen him in over a year and I was actually excited to hear from him. I got up and went to my living room with my laptop so that I could wait for Trei. While I was waiting I decided to do some advertising and promoting for our business grand opening.

I'm sure that we would do well but I was really trying to capture some of Meebles clients too without doing it illegally. I paid a couple different companies to run ads for the next two months and one to start after Valentine 's Day.

I know that sounds weird to you all but business picks up after you get intimate with someone and want to make sure that they are who they say they are. There are a lot of people with trust issues in this world and half of them have good reason.

Picking up my phone to video call Matt I noticed that I had a text from Trei. *Be there in 20 minutes.* I was excited. He was always in such a playful mood even when he was stressed the fuck out so it made me happy too.

Matt answered my video call wearing a worn out look on his face. I almost panicked but I noticed that he was at the park and it looks like he had just been running the trail.

"Oh I'm sorry for interrupting you but I was touching base with you about the business ads."

"I trust your work. If I didn't we wouldn't be partners now would we?" He said wearing a grin.

"I love the way that sounds. Partner."

"That's what I like to hear! We can meet tomorrow for a briefing before we dedicate time to those assholes at the firm. Right now I'm going to give this track my last bit of energy."

We both started laughing and said our goodbyes. Now that I had wasted a few minutes my nerves kicked in. Why was I nervous? It's not like me to be nervous so I turned to my go to for a calming of my nerves.

As I applied my lavender essential oil on my temples and nose I heard a car pull up and it was Trei. But when I saw him get out of the car I damn near orgasmed. This man was fucking sexy! I was starting to feel like the world's biggest slut but what no one knew was fine with me because this man was about to be mine.

Chapter Twenty Seven

Malik

I had made it home to an upset Yvette. Damn if it wasn't one it was the other. "What's wrong with you?"

"What were you doing that you couldn't answer your phone? I called you three times Malik."

"Damn, I was working. Trying to make money to pay for this wedding then I went to meet the man about my tuxedo. You really that mad over nothing?"

She turned around to face me quick. "Yes I am. You were unaccounted for and we can't start no marriage with disappearing acts."

Is she fucking serious?! "What the fuck you mean disappearing acts? And I'm not a child for you to keep tabs on."

She rolled her eyes and mumbled under her breath but I heard what she said anyway. "You act like a damn child though."

Next thing I knew I had choked her. I stopped as soon as I realized what I had done but the damage was done. She would never let me forget this act.

"I'm sorry Yvette. I'm really sorry. I snapped but you can't talk to me like that and you can't try to control everything. I am the man of this house and I go hard providing for you so I deserve a little respect."

Yvette was on the ground crying and I felt so bad for what I had done but she's lucky that's not my thing otherwise I would have put her ass to sleep. I hate a smart mouth and disrespectful female.

I went and sat on the couch with my head in my hands talking to myself. "How could you be so stupid? That was fucking stupid!" Then I looked up and there stood Yvette.

"I'm sorry Malik. I was a little upset because I'm nervous about the wedding and I let my thoughts run away today because I called your job and they said you left early."

I shook my head. Out of all the days for her to call me at work why today. "First of all they hate when we get outside calls so they wouldn't have called me to the phone anyway and I didn't leave work. I was on another job helping a coworker get his work load finished."

She began to cry harder. "I feel so stupid. I'm sorry bae and I forgive you."

Hearing that made me happy. I reached out and hugged her to let her know that we were good. "Next time talk to me and trust yo man. I do everything with you in mind. I would never do anything to hurt you."

That was a close call. I have to be more careful. But I almost lost two women in one day. What the fuck was going on? Maybe I needed to pull away from Jalyn a bit because marrying Yvette was definitely something I was going to do.

Letting everything settle down I decided to call it a night. I walked into the bathroom to prepare for a shower before bed. In the bathroom trash can I saw something strange. It looked like a condom. I carefully moved some things on top of it to the side. It's a muthafuckin condom!

Now I see why she was so upset that I didn't answer. This bitch needed to know when I was coming home so she wouldn't get caught. I got her ass. I decided not to notify her of my finding but I took a picture of it with my phone and jumped in the shower.

Here I was trying to wash another woman's scent off of me while trippin off of my woman cheating. Life is a trip. I'll have to play this one carefully because I wasn't losing Yvette either.

Getting out of the shower was hard to do because I knew that I had to face the woman that I love while keeping this information to myself. Shit was spinning out of control and I was the one letting it happen.

I had to focus so I texted Jalyn. *"I'm sorry that I wasn't honest with you but thank you for forgiving me. I ran into some issues at home and I need to take of things here but I could use your help."*

She texted back *"Sure"*. I know that she really didn't give a fuck about things at my house but I did. I needed to know that I was trippin. Yvette couldn't be cheating on me.

Next I texted Arman and told him that it was necessary that we talk tomorrow during the fittings. He responded with a guarantee to arrive earlier than the other guys. That's why he's my right hand man.

After all of the communicating was done I was tired. I turned to snuggle with Yvette but some time while I was on my phone she had crawled into bed and fell asleep already.

I wrapped my arms around her waist and kissed her shoulder then whispered "Goodnight my love." She was sound asleep and in ten minutes so was I. Tomorrow would be a better day. It had to be.

Chapter Twenty Eight

McKenzie

I couldn't have asked for a better night. 1800 in my system along with a margarita from earlier then Cordell showed up and showed out. He had this intense stare into my eyes while we had sex. I don't know what he was thinking but his performance was on point.

Knowing that I could be a handful I eased up on Cordell and told him to enjoy some time with his newborn. That was the best time to form that unbreakable bond with your baby. For the dad anyway. Moms get it from the start.

Now that I had time to myself I started doing some soul searching and decided that I wanted to do better for myself financially. Don't get me wrong I made good money at my job but I wanted more. I wanted my own too.

In the past I desired owning a gift shop. Not your average gift shop though. A novelty shop with adult gifts if you get my drift. From books to butt molding kits. Yeah that was my dream.

As I looked into those options I got help from those that I knew wouldn't do me wrong. A few did some research for me that yielded some great resources. I had a plan that I was going to put into motion and nothing was going to hold me back.

Three weeks had gone by faster than I realized and now I was the one too busy for Cordell. I could tell that he didn't like it but I was on a mission to be my own boss and like I said nothing nor anyone was going to stop me.

Although it was strange to me that sex was no longer on my mind even though that's technically what I was trying to sell. My boo crossed my mind but it wasn't dire like before.

I thought it was just because I was focused on my work. My friend Pedro seemed to think it was something more. He was one of my good friends that were helping to get my business plans together.

"Ma I'm telling you when my wife got pregnant she closed up shop for damn near two months before she got her mojo back."

I laughed so hard my stomach was now hurting. Although it didn't take much for my stomach to hurt lately he was making some serious faces while talking about his lack of sex.

"Pedro it's more reasons to lose a sexual appetite than a baby. The sex is what puts it there in the first place." I was trying to reason with him but he wasn't having that.

"All I'm saying is a home pregnancy test wouldn't hurt ma."

He was right. I told him to stop so that we could go into the drug store to pick up a test. Even though I knew that me and Cordell had missed using a condom a few times I knew that I wasn't having a baby.

In no way was I having a baby with a man that already had a family. Once we got the test Pedro was hitting the food strip as I called it. There was a stretch of Page that had a ton of restaurants on it and I was craving food.

Shit the more that I think about it I displayed some symptoms but again I knew I wasn't pregnant just hungry as hell.

"Pedro! Stop over there!"

Pedro damn near jumped out of his skin when I yelled for him to stop over at Rally's. This was by far my favorite burger fast food joint. Hands down favorite and I craved some now.

He pulled into the drive – thru and I swear I tried to order the whole damn menu. There wasn't a thing on the menu that I didn't want or eat. We finally decided on more than enough food and headed back to my house.

Once we arrived back at my house Pedro had to leave to attend to his family. He was such a loyal father, husband, and friend that's why I loved his crazy ass. He was my no hold back male friend of the year.

I tore into my food like there was no tomorrow eating everything that I could stomach. But my stomach had other plans. There was this feeling brewing in my gut that I knew wasn't going to be good.

That's when it hit me. I went running for the nearest thing which was the trash can. All of my precious Rally's came back up with a vengeance. This really was starting to take a toll on me mentally.

Now I was praying hard that what Pedro was saying wasn't true. Not now. Not with him. Lord knows I wasn't ready yet and especially when I had just got the courage to start a business.

First thing in the morning I would be taking that pregnancy test. Until then my nerves were everywhere because if I was I wouldn't be telling a soul about this. Like I said I wouldn't be having a baby with a man that already has a family.

Chapter Twenty Nine

Jalyn

Trei got out of his Range Rover looking so fucking delicious. I know that this was supposed to be a casual visit but I was turned on already. His once clean baby face was now covered in a full beard and goatee. It was so sexy on him.

I opened the door and welcomed him inside. His smile told me that he missed me before his words said it.

"What's up baby? Damn I missed you." He was hugging me so tight but I didn't want him to let go.

"Hey babe. Where have you been stranger? How has life been to you?"

"Life has been one ride after the other but it wasn't any fun because you weren't there by my side. Oh and I have a daughter."

"Wait...What!?!   You have a daughter? Congrats on the little blessing."

He looked at me and smiled before saying "Shit looks like I'm ready for another one." And just like that I hopped into his arms while he grabbed me up.

We made it over to the kitchen counter where he sat me down and pulled his dick out. Oh my gosh that muthafucka was huge! It's so thick and long that he was literally stretching me open.

His strokes felt so heavenly and his tongue was so sweet and thick in my mouth. This man made me forget everything and everybody. I continued to moan his name while whispering into his ear.

"Trei don't stop. I've missed you so much. Make your pussy cum baby."

The more I whispered into his ear and licked his earlobe the harder he went. I was loving it. Lost in his dreamy eyes and mesmerized by his savage yet Kingly presentation. I fucking loved this man.

Yeah I loved him but he never stuck around long enough for me to make him mine. I was praying that this time would be different. After going at it on the counter I wanted to feel him for real.

I hopped down off of the counter and bent over grabbing my ankles. He already knew what to do. I felt him enter me and it felt like losing my virginity all over again. Trei started off slow letting me throw it back at him and control the rhythm then he slowly began to pick up the pace.

My mind was gone. I could hear me yelling but I wasn't in control anymore. "Yes daddy!

Fuck me Trei. Oh God I'm coming!" Then I heard him say "Damn I missed my pussy."

He continued by saying "Tell me where to cum baby. Can I cum in this wet pussy?"

"Yes daddy! Please do!"

And just like that I felt him unload his load into me. I can't lie it felt fucking great. I didn't care about any consequences right now because I was just happy that he was back.

After we had finished he turned me around and kissed me like never before. "I'm back baby." That's all that he said as we held each other for what seemed like forever.

I pulled away long enough for him to fire up his blunt and follow me to the sitting room. This was my real living room that was located in the back of the house. This is where I chilled at the most.

He sat down and pulled me into his lap blowing smoke in my face. He knew that I smoked but not as much as him. I couldn't keep up with his blow schedule but I used to try.

See Trei was a street nigga and I loved him because I felt like I could truly be me whenever he was around and he loved it. No need to stay on point and be the smart black girl that everyone required me to be. I was just Jalyn.

I felt safe and secure in his arms. Shortly after we got settled on the sofa he kissed my neck and said again "I'm back for good this time. Nothing is going to keep me away from you this time. Nothing."

Although I loved hearing him say that I feared the last word. *Nothing.* I knew that when he made a promise that he meant it. But was I ready to shake Malik? How could I get rid of him when we had been friends for so long?

This was going to be hard. I wasn't worried about being business partners with Matt but he would have to stand down with his feelings if Trei was back to stay. The fact that I went from no love interest to three was really something I wasn't prepared for.

I had some real soul searching to do. I loved LaTrei first and Malik second but each love was so different. Then there was Matt whom I loved but not on that level.

For now I decided that Trei was here with me in my arms and that's who I was going to focus on because he was the one that kept getting away. Besides I needed to make my presence known in his life now that he had a child and baby momma.

I was about to let the real Jalyn out of the box. It was time that people played by my rules or it was game over.

Chapter Thirty

Malik

After my fucked up night I had taken time to myself and focused on work but today I needed to see Jalyn. She had agreed to help me find some truth behind the condom in my bathroom.

Yeah some time had passed since all of this but I required answers before walking down the aisle. Yvette seemed happy and all but my mind often wondered if she had let another man violate her body.

I know that was wrong of me to think considering the fact that I had been with another woman but two wrongs don't make a right.   Besides she didn't know about my wrong doings.

Jalyn hit me up saying that she was free and that I could come by her home office today at noon.   I was at work but I would have to make it some kind of way because I had to put this to rest.

My boss was a cool guy so I told him that I had wedding shit to tend to and he let me go early.   It really did both us some good since I was already over in time and was just letting the money stack by being there.

I jumped in my car and headed up I-70 to I-270 to Jalyn's house.   As I was headed to her house she texted me.   I was shocked to read that she no longer wanted me to use my key to enter.   Why the sudden change?

Anyway I would respect her wishes and call her when I got there.   I had so much on my mind that I think I sped the entire ride because I was there in fifteen minutes.   Normally it takes me longer to get to her house because she was secluded in the county.

Respecting her wishes I called and told her that I was outside. She came to the door looking so radiant. She was glowing from head to toe and the slim pantsuit that she was wearing was showing off her assets real nicely.

"You look nice baby."

"Thank you. So what's up?"

That wasn't what I was expecting from her. Nah, normally she would be floating on clouds hearing me call her baby. For some reason that did something to her and I didn't understand it but I loved it.

But today she was all business with me. She kept everything professional as I told her the details of my find and asked her to detail my fiancé. Her behavior made me feel like I should be paying so I offered.

"Well Malik I didn't ask for your money but if you want you can make a donation to a children's foundation of your choice on behalf of Leigh & Clay."

"Wow! So you really did it. You two started your own firm. I'm proud of you. Of course I'll donate to celebrate that special occasion."

I stood to give her a hug and a kiss and even that felt different. I know that we had been talking about Yvette but I didn't expect her to be giving me the cold shoulder.

So I grabbed her up and kissed her. This time she didn't pull away. She embraced me and kissed me back. This was my baby. This was what I wanted to feel. I guess asking my side chick to help fix shit with my fiancé was stupid in a lot of ways.

Now that I had her attention I held on to her and talked while embracing her. She talked to me about work and starting her own business with her ex dick in a box Matt.

After I felt like we were on good terms I tried to take her to lunch but she said that she had clients coming through today. I was happy to see that she was getting back to work so I left her to it.

I was happy all the way around the board because she had opened an investigation into my situation to see if I was trippin or not. I was praying that I was just nervous because of my own demons.

In no way could I handle hearing that my love was spreading her love to other men. That would devastate me because I always looked at her as being so pure. My mind was racing.

I needed a drink so I called up Arman to meet me at our favorite bar. Even though we had talked before the tuxedo fittings I hadn't told him about the condom. Maybe I would if it turned out to be something but for now it was my secret.

Arman agreed to meet up at the bar so I finished up some errands since I was off early then met Arman. He was there with his listening skills ready but this time I didn't have much to say. For some reason I wasn't feeling the whole spill my guts scenario so we played pool instead.

My life had been in such a whirlwind lately and I was beginning to wonder what was going on. Who could I trust? Who was really there for me? What was my purpose? All of these things were weighing heavy on my mind.

Hopefully Jalyn's conclusion would help me get my life back on track.

Chapter Thirty One

McKenzie

I woke up bright and early due to the storm brewing in my belly. "Oh God not this mess!" Those were the words leaving my mouth as I ran to the toilet. As soon as I finished puking my life away I pulled the test from the bathroom drawer.

After destroying the box and reading the instructions I was ready to find out my next move would need to be. I took the test and impatiently waited for the results.

As I waited I began to wash my face and disrobe. I wanted nothing more than to relax in a hot steamy shower right now so I prepared the water. Now I was sitting watching the lines form on this stick.

Moments later I burst into tears. "Why me? I'm not ready." The results were in and I was pregnant. With all of my emotions running loose my stomach became upset all over again.

I cried and vomited for the next ten minutes before crawling into the shower that was waiting for me. There I just stood hoping that the water would somehow wash away what was inside of me.

This was terrible. In no way could I be a baby momma. That thought made me think about Cordell and how happy he would be if I told him. More tears now rolled down my face.

Yes I loved him but I just couldn't do it. After spending some time relaxing in the water I washed my body and hair then hoped out of the shower. I wanted to call Cordell to tell him. I wanted to cry on his shoulder but I couldn't.

This was going to be something that I did on my own.

I headed into my kitchen to prepare some breakfast for me and this human growing inside of me. Damn. I was already thinking like a damn mom. Shaking my head at myself I started laughing out loud.

"Oh Mac what the hell did you get yourself into now?" I prepared eggs, grits, sausage, and an English muffin then sat to eat. Now I knew that I was pregnant because this was a lot of food sitting in front of me.

I decided to share my food so I went through my contacts to find a worthy breakfast buddy. Not a damn soul was worthy except Pedro and Jalyn. I picked Jalyn.

"Hello"

"Good morning girl. I made breakfast but it's entirely too much food would you like to come eat before work?"

"Umm I would but I'm a little busy at the moment."

I heard her laugh then it made me pay attention to the fact that she was breathing a little harder than usual.

"Bitch are you fucking right now?!"

"Uh yes and I really need to call you back! Be at your house shortly! Byyyyeee!"

I burst out laughing. This chick was wild. That was the Jalyn I had friended not the square that settled with Matt. Don't get me wrong he was cool to pass the time but definitely not her type.

Now I couldn't wait for her to bring her ass here. I had reason to get up and get dressed because she had details to share when she got here. Something had clicked in her and had sent her back to her old roots and I was diggin the change.

Making my way to my closet I looked at all of my bodycon dresses and belly shirts. I was not ready to give those up yet. I had to make me a doctor's appointment ASAP.

I called Dr. Bess and made an appointment for two weeks from today. This was going to be a long two weeks but at least I made the appointment. Sad thing was that this was just an appointment to find out all of the details.

Not wanting to think about all of stress that was brewing in me I turned on some tunes and started cleaning as I waited for freak nasty to get here. Two songs later my phone rings and interrupts my jam before I could even get going good.

I looked at the screen and it was Cordell. "Not right now baby daddy I'm jamming." I had to laugh at my own ignorance. This was the reason I was not ready to be a mom. My mouth and thoughts were unfiltered.

Half an hour had gone by before Jalyn showed up. I was happy to see her until I actually saw her. My once conservative friend looked so different. When I opened the door I saw a totally different person.

"Who the fuck are you?" She laughed at my question or maybe it was the shock on my face. Jalyn was wearing blue J's, white leggings that showed all of her ass, a blue V-neck graphic tee, with fire red bouncy curls.

"I'm me Mac. What you mean?"

We stared at each other for a minute before laughing and I moved to let her in. I jokingly said "Malik must be putting in work on that ass." But her smiled turned to a frown quick. Guess I fucked up.

Chapter Thirty Two

Cordell

It had been a while since I spent some time with Mac but those were her wishes. I had tried to entice her with dick pics but she wasn't having that. I even sent her a video of it coming and no action from her.

I was thinking that maybe it had something to do with me having a baby or spending time around Alese lately. Whatever it was I was going to rectify the problem. We had unfinished business.

I decided that today Mac was going to let me spend time with her no matter what. Picking up my phone I called her then sent her a sweet good morning text. I knew that she up because she was an early riser plus I had seen her activity online this morning.

She didn't know that I watched her page. Hell I don't even know if she would care but I wanted to watch the actions of these dogs out here trying to hit on her. They were some thirsty ass bums always begging for her to hit them up.

My baby text me back and it seemed that she was in a better mood today. I got hearts and kissey faces back with my good morning. Shit I was ready to pounce on her but I had to play it cool.

I asked her if she had time to talk and she replied that I should just come by her house if I was free. That's what the fuck I'm talking about! I missed this woman and I needed her in many ways.

Things were okay between Alese and I but it was something about Mac that drove me crazy.

Maybe it was her maturity. Maybe it was her smile. Or maybe it her long red hair that was always on point.

I don't know what it was but she was my Queen. She just didn't know it yet. I hoped in the shower to get ready to see Mac. She had taken the day off and I was trying to have her calling off tomorrow too.

After getting dressed I kissed my princess goodbye and was on my way to McKenzie. I was more excited than a kid in a candy store. Halfway there Alese calls me. I sent her to voicemail.

This was my time with my baby and she was not about to guilt trip me into coming back to her. As a matter of fact she needed to be going home. We could co-parent from different houses.

I walked up to the door of Mac's house but before I could ring the bell another red head opened the door. Damn she was thick as fuck. Who the fuck is she?

She snapped her fingers waking me from my trance. "Hi I'm Jalyn. You must be Cordell." The red head was extending her hand for a handshake.

"Yeah, I'm Cordell. Nice to finally meet the mysterious Jalyn."

She laughed and said "Well I'm off to work McKenzie. I'll call you later. Nice to meet the mysterious Cordell."

I shook my head and entered the house. Mac walked her friend out to her car as they laughed like little school girls. I stood watching because I knew what her friend looked like from some pictures on Mac's page but she looked damn good in person.

This chick had changed in a lot of good ways. I had to snap myself out of those thoughts. I was here for Mac. That was my baby. Besides I already had my hands full at home and these two were too close for any of that. But I wondered if they would link up.

Once my baby came back in the house I kissed her sexy lips then let my hands trace her hips. Oh how I missed her full hips and big ass. She wrapped her arms around my neck and pulled herself up into my arms.

I caught her and carried her over to the couch to give the neighbors a show because the curtain was wide open. I didn't care I had missed her. As soon as my lips touched her thigh she moaned. This was what I needed to hear.

Things took off from there and it felt so good. I could tell that she missed me too because she was wet as fuck. Now I could get back to my plan. I was trying to get a baby out her. I was going to keep giving her every drop of me until I got what I wanted.

We moved from the living room to the kitchen to the bedroom and finished in the garage. I don't even know how we ended up out there but no room was off limits today. Mac was exhausted from throwing it back so much so I put her in the bed and laid with her.

When she was sound asleep I went into the bathroom to clean myself up and go get lunch for when she awoke. Something caught my eye as I entered the bathroom. Is this what I think it is?

I don't know if she meant for me to see this or not but I was happy to find it. Right there on the ledge of the bathtub was a pregnancy test that displayed a positive reading. Not being able to contain myself I ran back into the room and woke her up.

But the tears that exploded from her eyes when she saw what I was holding told me that I was the only one happy about this news.

Now I felt like shit. I prayed that I could change her mind.

Chapter Thirty Three

Jalyn

I had been feeling good with Trei spending nights here with me. Nights with me made for some really good mornings. This particular morning Mac called and caught me in the act.

Normally I don't answer the phone while engaged in intercourse but he dared me to do it. Thank God it was McKenzie. So after Trei left for work I headed to my friend house for breakfast. This was indeed a good morning.

Although I was heading to work myself I had a lunch date with LaTrei so he chose my wardrobe this morning. I was feeling the comfort level of it but I knew others would have something to say.

It was simple but it brought out the old Jalyn not the book smart business woman that everyone knew. I loved it though. And my thoughts were right because when I got to McKenzie's house she flipped out.

We laughed about it but of course I had to explain my outfit choice. "What's wrong with my outfit? My baby picked it out for me to wear today. This is what he wanted to see me in when we have our lunch date today."

"Your baby? That's what's up. But a lunch date? Fool be careful. He is about to be a married man and you're going out in public with him like this."

She was grabbing her boobs and butt as she said this. But my face must have had a bad expression on it because she continued talking.

"Don't be mad Jay I'm just looking out for you.   We don't need problems from Ms. Wannabe."

"Slut I'm not mad about that per say.   I'm mad that you think I'm talking about Malik being my baby."   I said as I started laughing. Now she was super confused.   I hadn't told her that Trei was back.

"Huh?! Explain."

I told her how I got the call from LaTrei and how he showed up that night.   Then I filled her in on everything that had happened in between then and now.   Her mouth was open the entire time.

"Now I see why I haven't heard from you and why you're dressed like this."

"Like what? I think that I look good."

"EXACTLY! That's the point. You look good not all business all of the time. Shit keep his ass here for a lengthy period this time."

We both laughed but she had a point. I needed him to stick around for a while so I sent him a text.

Me: Babe I really hope that you stick around this time. Don't leave me. I LOVE YOU!

Trei: Baby I'm all yours but my daughter needs me too.

Me: Oh...I see

Trei: Look I love you more baby and I'm yours but I need my princess too. I promise to come back.

Me: So let's do this...together

I put my phone away and continued to talk to Mac for a while before saying that I needed to head to work.

"You're going to work in that?"

"Yes, is there a problem?"

"It will be when you get to your firm." She said laughing and holding her stomach.

"Whatever. Can I take the rest of breakfast to go? I have a client that wants me to watch his wife. He thinks she's cheating yet he's cheating himself."

"How do you know that? What you fucking clients now?"

She was joking but I was or had fucked a client and my business partner. That was crossing the line one too many times.

"Actually, yes. His name is Malik."

"Are you serious?"

"Dead ass"

We both fell over laughing. I hugged her, grabbed the breakfast she had packed for me, and headed to the door. Just then her boo thang was about to enter so I was happy to be leaving.

Now I was off to do my surveillance work. This was going to be a challenge since she did know who I was and what I looked like but I'm good at my job. I got this.

I texted Malik for him to check in with her and he did. So I headed to their home since that's where she was claiming to be. When I got there I was shocked to see that there was indeed someone there with her but who?

Chapter Thirty Four

Malik

The day had finally come for Jalyn to start her assignment for me. I was nervous as hell. Part of me wanted answers and the other half hoped that she wouldn't find anything wrong.

She had texted me in the morning asking me to check in with Yvette to see where she was. Now I was at work patiently awaiting some sort of feedback. I trusted Jalyn to do the job because she was sharp with her details.

Jalyn wasn't just sexy she was smart as fuck too. I loved everything about her. Those thoughts started to make me feel some type of way about hiring her to do this job. Maybe I was wrong.

It also made me feel some type of way that my feelings were so strong for her yet I was definitely marrying someone else. My thoughts were interrupted by the sound of text messages coming thru.

They were from Yvette. She was sending me explicit pictures. I can't say it was out of character but it was unexpected. Why put on lingerie at nine o'clock in the morning knowing that I won't be home until four o'clock.

I wanted to leave work so bad but I knew that Jalyn was on the job right now so I had to trust her. I send a text back to Yvette telling her to save it for later and her text simply read okay.

My mind was wondering who was there with her so I texted Jalyn to ask if she had anything for me. She reported that someone was definitely at my home but she didn't know who yet.

Now I was furious. I called Jalyn. I told her what Yvette had just done and at first she was silent but then she erupted in laughter. I didn't see anything funny but I couldn't be mad at her. My side chick shouldn't be watching my fiancé anyway.

She said "Calm down I'll stay here until the police show up telling me to move or I see who's at your house. But just so you know I hope he fucked her just as good as you fucked me."

"Why the fuck would you say some stupid shit like that?" I was beyond heated at this point.

"Because Malik you are wrong on many levels so take the bass out of your fucking voice! I fucking hate you right now. You spend days at my house but you can never take me where I'd like to go because of what?

Oh yeah your girl. You fuck the life out of me on a daily but that's all that I get from you."

The line went silent but we were both still there. Then she spoke "I deserve better. I left better for you."

I was speechless. She had used so many hurtful words that I didn't care what was going on at my home anymore. I had to fix this shit immediately. Hearing her say these things to me broke me down.

There was no way that I could stay at work like this so I left. I asked Jalyn to meet me at her house and she said no. I wouldn't take that for an answer so I left work anyway in hopes that she would meet me.

She stood her ground saying that she was on an assignment and that she never abandons a job. After a while she stopped replying to me and no longer answered my calls.

I fucked up. But now I understood why she was so distant from me. My baby hated me. That hurt so bad. I drove like a mad man all the way home. Once I pulled up Jalyn pulled off leaving me even more hurt and to deal with the drama in my house by myself.

Taking a look at the car in my driveway I knew who it was. No need for alarm because it was just Yvette's friend Shaila. I thought about trying to go to Jalyn's house but instead I went in my own home.

I opened the door and didn't see anyone in the front of the house but I heard them. I heard them moaning. Already feeling fucked up I thought that I was imagining things.

Nah I was hearing female moans so I quietly closed the door and followed the sounds. I'll be damned if I didn't find Yvette bent over letting her friend fuck her with a strap on. What the fuck was I here for?

She didn't notice me walk in the room. They were straight going at it and she was wearing the same lingerie that she had taken pictures in. That's who it was really for.

I took my phone out and started recording so that I would have proof of her wrong doings. Since they didn't see nor hear me enter I recorded enough footage and quietly walked away.

But when I left the house I made sure to slam the front door. I got back in my car and left not knowing where I was going. Did that explain the condom in the trash can? Was there still a nigga in the picture?

I sent the video to Jalyn and told her to add it to the case and consider it closed. That's when I got a text back from her. *"I would have included you. Good luck with that gold diggin bitch!"*

All that I could do was pull over to the shoulder and cry. My life wasn't shit.

Chapter Thirty Five

McKenzie

I had a great morning with my friend and my baby. He came through and took care of my body. Shit I didn't even know that I was missing him so damn much. Guess I had put that out of my mind.

Now he was staring at me with so much excitement in his eyes about the one thing that I didn't want him to know. Everyone had shown up so quick and all at once that I hadn't had time to get rid of that damn test.

I sat up in the bed and he sat next to me but facing me. This was not what I was expecting.

"Look Cordell I just found out this morning and I really didn't know what to say or do."

"McKenzie you know that I'll take care of you and the baby with no problems."

"Yeah but I don't know if I'm ready for all of that Cordell."

My words must have cut him deep because his smile had disappeared that quickly and he was now staring at me with watery eyes.

"So you were just going to kill my baby without talking to me! How fucking dare you? I'll be damned if you destroy what's mine because of your selfish ass ways. I'm the father of that fetus and we will be having a baby McKenzie."

"I'm selfish? Nigga you better sit yo ass down somewhere! You have a bitch at YOUR house right now with a one month old so who the fuck is selfish now?!"

I was beyond mad and he knew it. Now he was trying to grab me and calm me down for the sake of the baby. What he didn't know was that all of this was really making me not want a child with him.

Life would be just fine without him if he chose to leave me. Hell he wasn't really mine anyway. I had a life ahead of me that no one was going to ruin. Cordell was losing it as I got up and got dressed.

There was nowhere in particular that I was going but I wanted to get far away from him right now. He started to speak and I wasn't interested until I saw that he was on his knees crying.

"Get the fuck up Cordell. Listen to me when I say that you don't call the shots around here. So don't come up in my house talking shit to me especially when you're in the fucking wrong."

"I'm sorry baby but you don't realize how happy this made me. You still don't get that I love you so fucking much. I'm trying to be the best man that I can be for you right now yet you keep me at arm's length."

"STUPID, BECAUSE YOU HAVE A WOMAN!"

He got up off of his knees and headed towards me wiping his eyes. I won't lie it tore me apart to see him like this because now I knew that he really wanted this child.

Cordell walked up to me and hugged me tight. He said between tears "I understand the situation that I put you, I mean us, in. But know that I'll always be there for you no matter what. I love you and without a doubt I would love our child. Please just give it thought but if you make your move then so be it."

Just like that he kissed me on my forehead, grabbed his coat, and headed out of the door. I was relieved yet traumatized because I swore that I wouldn't tell anyone so now I was alone with my thoughts.

I called Cordell's phone and told him to come back. He did. After a minute of not saying anything I sat as close as I could to him. "Cordell I love you and it hurts that you mislead me. Now I'm pregnant and feel like I'm going to be alone. This isn't how I pictured starting a family."

"I understand that Mac but we're a family nonetheless."

We talked for a while about what to do next and ended the conversation with a kiss. Next I went back to the bedroom to get some sleep because I was feeling exhausted. He followed me

He stripped out of his clothes and joined me in bed. I really had been missing this feeling. I tried to turn toward him but he had me pinned down with his arm.

He whispered in my ear "I've been waiting on this for a while." Then he started playing in my wetness for round two and I was ready. I had been missing that dick because I was craving it like crazy now.

I pulled away long enough to get some lube and shook the bottle at him. "You ready for some real fun big boy?"

His eyes lit up, "You mean what I think you mean?"

I shook my head yes and tooted my ass up in the air. The rest was history. He went in on my ass but it felt so good. Nothing but moans and heavy breathing could be heard throughout the entire house.

True I hated not being his only but I wasn't ready to lose him altogether either. And after this round he wasn't going to be able to keep me off of his mind.

Chapter Thirty Six

Jalyn

Malik had some nerve to think that I gave a fuck about his bitch being in bed with another bitch. It serves him right too. Out of all of the private investigators out there he asked me to watch his wife. Fuck him.

I was really starting to let the hateful feelings that I was suppressing for him surface. He deserved it though. He ran around acting like he was the muthafuckin man when he was nothing more than a hoe.

Yeah I guess some of my feelings at the moment came from him not giving me all of his love. Telling me that he was in love with me yet he proposed to her days before expressing feelings for me.

But oh well I was a fool once but not anymore. That half a year that we had did feel special but only because I blocked out his real life. I made me his wife when he was around. I was fucking stupid.

Although I never thought that he would do me like that it wasn't a surprise. And thank God I didn't have to worry about going back to him because I was chasing the one that was in my bed every morning and night.

Trei was the one that I really wanted to spend my life with. He loved me for me and I needed that. Between my savage attitude right now thanks to Malik and my baby Trei around I had a new attitude.

Since I had officially done my job I had free time so I made my way to Matt's house to inform him of the open and closed case. When

I got there he had a client so I stayed in my car.

Once the man left I got out and the look of disappointment on Matt's face was priceless. He had never seen me dressed so urban and I guess it wasn't his thing.

I walked up to him and said "Well hey there partner." He let his eyes follow me into the house but never said a word. Then I heard the door close. When I turned to talk to him he was standing right behind me.

Matt kissed me and tried to put me on his dining room table but I backed away. "I'm sorry. I didn't mean to upset you."

"It's okay Matt, seriously."

"It's just that I didn't know what to make of your attire at first but I must admit it makes your body look fucking amazing."

I couldn't be mad at his reaction. I ignored what he was saying and started to share the information about the job that I had done. "I'll fax or bring you the paperwork when I get all finished up."

"Thank you." He managed to say.

Matt stood there staring at me before speaking again. "Thank you for being a great partner. We haven't even moved into the space completely yet you are already on the job. This is why I wanted you on my team. You are a phenomenal woman Jalyn."

"Thank you Matt and I am more than grateful to be your partner. Never doubt that. I will get the job done no matter what."

With that being said I walked to the door and left. Now it was time to go have lunch with my baby. I would be a little early but I didn't care. Watching him work turned me on.

Especially when he was working hard and his muscles flexed through his shirt. Whoo! That man did something to me. Just thinking about him had me ready to pull over and pleasure myself.

I texted Trei that I was on my way and he texted back letting me know that he was ready for me. This was what I wanted every day. To have someone that was mine and could be seen with me in public places was great.

The feeling that I got when I arrived at his job was even better. He met me at my car and picked me up swinging me around while he hugged me. Then he put me down and kissed me.

That felt so good to have someone share their love with not just me but whoever was watching. I ate that moment up. Trei and I ate lunch while we just talked and played around.

Our relationship came up during the talk and Trei told me that he would love me forever. He said that he wanted me to meet his daughter and be a part of her life. That gave me such a great feeling. I wanted that too.

As we wrapped up lunch he told me that I would be his wife one day and have his child. I was beaming with every word that he said to me. No one knew that I wanted a child to love and spoil because I was just figuring this out myself.

If I was going to have a family it would definitely be with this man. I leaned into his ear and whispered "Let's work on that baby now". That was all that I had to say.

He looked around for a secure spot before saying fuck it and took me into his arms right there up against his truck. The rush from possibly being spotted was great. It was a high I couldn't explain even if I tried.

This man had me changing who I was mentally and physically. I was falling in love and   enjoying   it.

Chapter Thirty Seven

Malik

After having a breakdown in my car I headed back to my house to confront the two of them. Sure enough they were still there. I entered the house but this time I headed straight for the bedroom with the camera rolling.

They hadn't finished so I caught them in the act for the second time. As I entered the room Yvette was on her knees sucking on this dirty bitch clitoris like her life depended on it.

Shit she never sucked me like that, I was mad about that. Shaila was laid back on the bed with her hands wrapped in my fiancé hair. She looked up and saw me.

"Oh shit!" She jumped up and away from Yvette.

"Calm down. I've already been here once today and saw you fucking my wife with your fake dick."

"Baby let me explain!"

"What's to explain Yvette? You're a hoe. I am marrying a hoe. You can get down on your knees to lick a bitch pussy but you give me hell about sucking my dick."

They were both staring at me in pure shock. So I continued.

"Then I saw you take a big ass dildo up the ass. You were straight moaning over some plastic but won't fuck me like that. You don't do shit but lie there like a bump on a log when I'm trying to fuck. You're a confused hoe."

By now Shaila was trying to console Yvette as she was crying hard. I guess I had hurt her feelings but fuck all of that she was wildin.

"Aye look y'all need to be get the fuck out. I need to think and clean my sheets and shit from y'all funky ass shenanigans."

"Look you can't keep talking to her like that she is your fiancé." Yelled the wrong fucking person

I walked up on this poorly built chick and told her through clenched teeth "Or what bitch?"

The fear in her eyes was priceless. She walked away and grabbed Yvette by the arm. I yelled behind them "That's right take your girlfriend with you. She don't do shit around here anyway!"

I could hear Yvette big crying as she got dressed in the living room to leave. I had been nice for too long and with everything that just happened I wasn't in a caring mood.

This was draining. I sent Jalyn a text telling her that I was sorry and that I really did care about her. I wasn't expecting a response but that's something that I needed to do for me.

After I had text Jalyn I texted Yvette telling her not to contact me until I contacted her. I told her that I would put that video on the internet for all to see and sell it to a porn site if she did. I meant business too.

She didn't respond. Probably out of fear but it was cool with me. I stripped the sheets off of the bed and laid down on the bare bed. I didn't care about anything right now but sleep.

When I woke up from my much needed nap I checked my phone. I had a missed call from Jalyn and a text too. She had decided that we needed to talk in person and I was okay with that.

I texted her to meet me at my house whenever she could because I had cleaning to do. I didn't know if she didn't like what I said or what because she never responded. Then an hour later I saw her sexy ass.

She was matching her car today and with all that was going on I hadn't noticed that she had dyed her hair fire red. Damn she was sexy. I couldn't lose her. I hope she felt the same way.

Jalyn walked in and took a seat at the breakfast counter. She reached for a glass and held it up as to say fill it up. I poured her up some Tequila straight and sat down next to her.

"Jalyn I'm sorry for everything. I'm sorry for how I made you feel. That was never my intentions and you should know that."

"I don't assume anything Malik. And even though you told me how you feel your actions told me a bigger story. But it's cool because we are friends and I don't want to throw that away just yet. We have a lot of work to do tho."

"I agree but I'm willing to put in that work. I promise."

We sat talking about our likes and dislikes within each other and drinking. Eventually we shared a few laughs which brought me to my next move. I stood next to her stool and grabbed her face.

I planted the most passionate kiss on her and I knew that it had her moist because she was a kisser. She loved kissing and being kissed. I knew I had her when she let out a soft moan.

She didn't fight. Instead she stood up and walked me backwards to the couch. I fell down onto the couch as I removed my shirt. Jalyn stood over me removing her clothes and exposing her dangerous curves and caramel skin that I wanted to devour.

As she began to kneel I grabbed the back of her head putting my dick in her mouth. She sucked on it savoring my dick and I knew why. She wanted to be free from me. She wanted this to be the end.

Her head was so good I had her stop to straddle me. Looking into her beautiful brown eyes and listening to her moan while her body glistened from our body heat sent me over the edge.

I bust not caring that I wasn't strapped. Hell I would love for her to conceive. I was trying to make this the beginning not the end.

Chapter Thirty Eight

McKenzie

Cordell had indeed being calling me more and stopping by my job to bring me lunch. He was showing me that he would be around. I liked that. Like I said I wasn't ready to lose him yet.

Besides that he was trying to change my mind and make me keep the baby. My appointment was today and I was nervous as hell. I told Cordell that he could come more for my support than the fact that this was his child.

He was there promptly. I walked in nervous of what was to come. Cordell whispered in my ear. "Baby relax. Everything is going to be just fine. I'm sure everything is okay with Jr."

That made me laugh out loud louder than I wanted to. He said "Oh you find that funny? So what you thought his name was going to be?"

"Who the hell says it's even going to be a boy? Just because you already have a girl means nothing to me. I don't."

"Oohh you sexy when you get all defensive and feisty."

We laughed again then he said "I don't care what we have. I'm just happy to hear that it seems like you'll be having my baby." He was wearing a huge grin on his face.

"You know what I guess that is what I'm saying."

He hugged me so tight I yelled "Ouch". This got us back into a room quicker too. I told Cordell "Over the last two weeks I've gotten used to watching what I do and eat and shit. Guess you can say the little peanut is growing on me. Literally growing."

"Baby I promise not to do you wrong. I also promise to tell Alese about us."

Whoa. I was shocked by that last part. I never asked him to do that and I'm not sure that I wanted her to know. This was too much right now.

"Slow down cowboy. Let's get our feet planted on solid ground before you go doing something like that. That's extreme."

He sat quietly for a while rubbing my barely big belly. I kissed him to let him know that everything was okay. We always sealed our conversations with a kiss anyway.

I heard the doctor approach the door and pick up my chart. Again I grew nervous. The door opened and in walked Dr. Bess. She was a short and chipper older woman. I actually liked her and trusted her work.

"Hi there Ms. Witts. And hi there Mr..." She extended her hand and waited for us to introduce Cordell.

"Hi I'm Cordell James."

"Nice to meet you Mr. James I am Denise Bess and I'll be taking care of Ms. Witts."

Cordell nodded and so did I. Dr. Bess asked what brought me in as if she didn't know so I explained everything that happened and led me to my discovery.

She laughed at my expressions because she knew that this was not something that I planned. Dr. Bess continued with her questions then asked me for a urine sample. I hated those.

I complied and returned to the room for more examining. There was so much touching that I thought they were trying to get me off. Shit I was ready to help them.

Once the doctor and nurse had completed their assessment I was off to an ultrasound. That's where I found out how far along I was. We were both shocked to learn that I was already two and a half months.

That meant that somewhere during our condom usage one broke. Long before we threw them out I was pregnant. Ain't that a bitch. These were the curveballs that life threw me.

They gave Cordell a printed image of the ultrasound just for his amusement. The excitement was so visible on his face. He really was excited to be having another child. I was falling in love more watching him today.

Then the evil thoughts crept into my mind. I wondered if he did all of this with her and if he was this excited for her to have his child.

Shaking my head I hoped to get rid of the thoughts hating on this joyful occasion.

Yes I said joyful. If having this man baby meant that he was happy then I knew that I would ultimately be happy. And as long as I kept him fed, fucked, and tired he wouldn't have time for her.

With the appointment over we gathered ourselves to return to the real world. Cordell was going back to work and I was off to fill the prescriptions that they had given me for nausea and my prenatal pills.

This was going to be a journey and I was now ready to share it with the world but first my close friends. Time for a gathering at my house to officially introduce Cordell into my world.

I couldn't wait to share this news with them because I knew that they would be shocked but would except and help me through this process. I loved my friends. Even the broke and ratchet ones.

Yeah this was about to be a big change and I was still going for my own business. When I told Cordell he was on board with the idea and wanted to help out however he could. At first I thought having a kid would be the end of me but this was about to be a great beginning.

Chapter Thirty Nine

Cordell

I had been trying hard to get Mac to keep the bundle of joy growing in her belly. I think it paid off. She was ready to announce to all of her friends that she was pregnant and she wanted me there to introduce me as the father.

Man I was so proud of her. I wouldn't miss this opportunity for the world. I didn't give a fuck who had something to say or my situation at home. Fuck all of that shit.

I was going to be there every step of the way for her and afterwards I would be there for both of them. This was the family that I wanted and I was ready to claim them as so.

My brother was the first person that I contacted when I found out that she would keep the baby. He seemed partial to the thought of me having another baby so soon and with someone that he didn't know shit about.

"Bruh I'm in love with her. She makes me feel shit that I don't and have never felt with Alese."

"Sooooo why the fuck are you still with the girl? Cut her loose bruh. She's young and can bounce back. Just do this shit right so we can keep visitation with our niece."

"Yeah I hear you big bruh. No matter what I will be in my daughter life. You already know how I get down."

"Yeah I do that's why I said do this shit right."

I knew what my brother meant by do it right. And nothing and no one was going to stop me from being a father to my children. That I can promise you. So bruh didn't need to worry.

Mac wanted to be more than just a mom now and I loved it. She wanted to work for herself in hopes of making it big and having time for her family. Yeah I keep saying family because that's what we were going to be one day.

I headed home to Alese and my daughter Brittani. I really don't know why I did that.

"Cordell we need to talk."

"What's up Alese?" I asked as I picked up my baby girl

"You spend a lot of time away from home now and I was wondering was it because we were here."

"Alese I been told you to go to your house and that I would co-parent the same as if you were here. You got my spot looking like a section 8 jumpoff."

"Fuck you Cordell! I don't have to stay here and take this shit." She was silently crying now.

"Besides Cordell I know that there's another female in the picture. I'm not stupid. You spend nights away from home. You come back smiling until you see me. I can tell that we're done."

It was kinda fucked up that she peeped all of that yet at the same time it made my next statement that much easier.

"You're right. There is someone else and she's pregnant. I care about her and you know that I care about that baby just like I care about Brittani. I'm going to be there no matter what."

"So does she know what you really do for work? Because I would hate for her to find out the hard way."

She was staring at me with hate in her eyes. They looked so dark and evil. I approached her still holding our daughter and looked right into her eyes. I didn't speak. I didn't have to.

Alese got the message loud and clear. "Don't get yourself in a situation that you can't get out of."

Her eyes widened. Alese knew what I did under the table and my legit job. Mac didn't know too much of either yet she knew that I made good money and was available when she needed me.

I was starting to get mad so I put the baby down in her bassinet. I went into spare bedroom that was being converted into a nursery. She followed me in and began questioning me again.

"Do you love her?"

"Yes, I'm in love with her."

A tear fell from her eye. I tried not to care.

"Are you going to brand her too?"

I looked at her for a while before answering "No, she's different."

Alese started crying and gathered her things. She walked back to kiss the baby and said to me "I love our daughter but I can't do this Cordell. I'd rather be a memory than watch some woman have what I wanted."

"What does that mean?"

She didn't respond to me. Instead she kissed the baby again and whispered that she loved her then walked out of the house. I watched her get into her car and drive away.

I didn't know that what she was about to do would be the beginning of a new world for me.

Chapter Forty

Jalyn

Today was a good day that went wrong real quick. I had been kissed by Matt, fucked my babe at work which was good as fuck, then met up with Malik and fucked him too.

That was not supposed to happen. I simply wanted to keep my friendship with him not keep him as a lover. Now here I was in his arms crying over feelings and shit.

"Malik I can't do this anymore. I can't be intimate with you after this. We have to be friends only."

"Baby I can't let you go. You are my world and I always turn to you when things go wrong. I need you"

While we were sitting there talking Trei called me. Sadly I had to ignore that call and text him instead.

Me: Hey babe I went back to work for an hour

Trei: Alright well I'm going to take care of some business but I'll be waiting on my Queen

Me: I'll be home soon my King

I loved this man so why was I here with Malik? I needed to get my ass home immediately. Getting up and trying to get myself together I saw Malik looking down.

"What's wrong?"

"Who was that?"

"None of your business."

"Are you seeing someone? I can't be mad if you are but I thought I was your everything?"

"And I thought I was yours."

"That hurt Jalyn. You are my everything I just can't explain my world right now. Hell my world fell apart earlier. I don't even know if I'm getting married."

"Well the damage is done Malik and it hurt really bad."

I walked into the bathroom and cleaned myself up and brush my teeth as I always did when I was here. Afterwards I got dressed and headed to my car. Malik never moved from his spot on the couch.

As I was walking out of the door I looked back one last time. He was now sitting with his head in his hands and if I didn't know any better I'd say that he was now crying.

A part of me wanted to console him and love him until he couldn't take it anymore but I knew that I would only be repairing him to go back to her. For whatever reason he loved her and wanted her in his life forever.

I left without saying a word and went home to my King. Trei might have been rough around the edges but he was my diamond in the rough and I loved it. He was all that I needed and he was willing to give me all that I needed. What more could I ask for?

When I walked through the door I saw the most precious sight. Trei was on the floor putting together a puzzle with his daughter. She was so adorable. I froze and pulled out my phone before he could move.

I got a picture of them and that's when they noticed I even entered the house. He jumped up with baby in tow and walked up to me giving me a kiss. She mimicked her daddy giving me a kiss on the cheek. This made me melt.

"I missed you baby"

"Oh yeah daddy? I thought you were pretty full after lunch."

He laughed and said "Nah I worked all of that off. I'm hungry."

I couldn't believe that he was talking about eating me while he was holding his daughter. Then I noticed that he had grabbed the huge print in his pants. Lord this man was well endowed.

"Is baby girl staying the night?"

"Only if her step mom wants her to."

"Step mom? I like that. Has a nice "ring" to it." I said as I wiggled my ring finger at him. He laughed and kissed me again. I told him that once she went to bed that we would definitely work on a little brother for princess.

He loved that idea. I was starting to love that idea myself. I was ready to settle down with a love of my own. Start a family of my own. I felt like I deserved to be happy.

Thoughts of what I had just done with Malik popped into my head and all of a sudden I felt sick. I got physically sick. Luck was on my side as I made it to the bathroom just in time.

I spent some time in there praying to God for any sign of what I should do and how to move past Malik. And just like that he answered my prayers. In crawls Maliha with a little black box.

As I opened it my eyes filled with tears instantly. I could barely see LaTrei stooped down before me. "Baby I wanted to do this so differently but I couldn't wait. I love you and I'm ready to make you mine forever. I'm ready to start a family with this beautiful woman before me. Will you please do me the honors of becoming Mrs. Jalyn Monroe Edwards?"

"Jalyn! Jalyn baby wake up!"....

Death of a Side Chick coming soon!

I hope that you enjoyed your read. If so be on the lookout for Death of a Side Chick! And as always I welcome your feedback and love reading your emails!

YaneeBrinks@gmail.com

Also By Yanee Brinks

Sip, Read, & Fantasize: Short Reads for the Adult Minds

Love, Hate, & Heartache Book of Poems

Love, Hate, & Heartache Book of Poems 2

Naughty Girl Poems